Ruthless Royal Sheikhs

Two royal brothers—
bound by duty, but driven by desire!

A born leader and a playboy prince…

But *nothing* is more important to Ilyas and
Hazin al-Razim than honouring
their royal birthright!

Until their searing passion for two beautiful
and fiery women challenges everything
they've ever known—and these Sheikhs
won't rest until they've claimed them!

Discover Ilyas and Maggie's story in

Captive for the Sheikh's Pleasure

Available now from
Mills & Boon Modern Romance!

And read Hazin and Flo's story in

Christmas Bride for the Sheikh

Available now from
Mills & Boon Medical Romance!

You won't want to miss this scorching duet
from Carol Marinelli!

Dear Reader,

I've been unfaithful!

Sheikh Prince Hazin al-Razim was born as the requisite 'spare', and I have to confess I fell more than a little in love with him while writing his brother Ilyas's story.

Ilyas, the Crown Prince, has the running of the country on his mind—whereas the next in line, Hazin, runs wild and apologises to no one.

He has his reasons, though, and they made me tear up several times while writing his story.

It was clear to me that this bad boy hero needed a very special heroine to tame him. Possibly someone who runs a little wild herself.

Well, along comes Flo, a gorgeous midwife, who attracts all the wrong sorts and has sworn off men. She's doing very well with that pledge until the night she meets Hazin!

I don't blame her a bit. :)

Happy reading!

Carol

CHRISTMAS BRIDE FOR THE SHEIKH

BY
CAROL MARINELLI

Published in Great Britain 2017
By Mills & Boon, an imprint of HarperCollins*Publishers*
1 London Bridge Street, London, SE1 9GF

© 2017 Carol Marinelli

ISBN: 978-0-263-07037-8

MIX
Paper from
responsible sources
FSC® C007454

This book is produced from independently certified FSC paper
to ensure responsible forest management. For more information
visit www.harpercollins.co.uk/green.

Printed and bound in Great Britain
by CPI Group (UK) Ltd, Croydon, CR0 4YY

Carol Marinelli recently filled in a form asking for her job title. Thrilled to be able to put down her answer, she put 'writer'. Then it asked what Carol did for relaxation and she put down the truth—'writing'. The third question asked for her hobbies. Well, not wanting to look obsessed, she crossed her fingers and answered 'swimming'—but, given that the chlorine in the pool does terrible things to her highlights, I'm sure you can guess the real answer!

Visit the Author Profile page
at millsandboon.co.uk for more titles.

CHAPTER ONE

I PROMISE I'LL be good.

Florence Andrews lay on her side beneath the sheets, with a heavy male arm pinning her, and promised that if the powers that be could possibly reverse the mistakes made last night then she would be good for the rest of her life.

'Morning,' he said sleepily, and she felt the morning swell of him on the back of her thigh. It was so insistent he might just as well have been prodding her to get up.

She said nothing, deciding it was far safer to feign sleep.

Flo was all too used to getting it wrong with men.

Petite, with blonde hair and china-blue eyes, Flo had found that she attracted a rather specific type of male— ones whose names began with a B and ended with a D.

Bad.

Bastard.

Either would fool her.

The last man she had dated had practically had to come with written references before she'd even agreed to go out with him, yet he had turned out to be just like the rest.

A louse.

In fact, even thinking of him had Flo screwing her eyes more tightly closed in shame.

She'd sworn off men, so it had been an awfully long time since she'd gone out with anyone.

Not that she and Hazin had ever *been out*. It hadn't even been a date.

She opened her eyes and the view of a cold, grey London in autumn was as stunning as it had been last night. Big Ben let her know it was just after eight and from the dizzy height of the presidential suite it looked like a black and white photo, except for the rain hitting the vast windows.

Flo knew she had outdone herself in the rake stakes this time.

Sheikh Prince Hazin al-Razim of Zayrinia came with warnings attached rather than references.

She knew his title, not because he had told her but because of her friend.

Well, she had actually known of him before Maggie had got mixed up with his brother. Scandalous photos of Hazin were plastered over the Internet. His handsome face and naked body—with a generous black rectangle covering the necessary—appeared from time to time in the trashy magazines that the mothers read on the maternity ward where she was a midwife.

They would sometimes even giggle with Flo about him.

His reputation was appalling. Hazin was completely irredeemable; in fact, he was bad to the bone.

Yet he was adored by all.

And last night he had been, without a shadow of doubt, the best lover of her life.

Hazin had either fainted from a lack of blood to the head or he was asleep again, because the arm that had been pulling her back was loose now on her stomach and his breathing was even.

It gave her a pause.

How long the peace would last, she could not be sure.

Did she tell him she knew who he was and explain how their seemingly chance meeting had come about?

Would there even be conversation, given all they had between them was sex?

How the hell had she got into this mess? Flo wondered as she lay there. She was supposed to have been helping out her friend!

Flo had no intention of going out this evening. Maggie had texted and asked if Flo could stop by at the café where Maggie worked. Her friend had brought a souvenir home from her backpacking trip around the world—she was six months pregnant.

By Crown Prince Sheikh Ilyas of Zayrinia!

'I have to tell him.' Maggie said as they lunched. 'But I don't know how to.'

Privately, Flo wasn't too sure that Maggie did *have* to tell the father.

Oh, she was all for parental responsibility, but her friend was her main concern and she was pregnant by a future King, no less!

The baby was due just after Christmas. But as well as that, Maggie had recently found out she was having a little boy, and Flo was concerned how that might impact the situation.

Still, it wasn't for Flo to decide and so she told Maggie what she knew.

'His brother will be at Dion's tonight.'

'How do you know?'

'Because he gets kicked out of there every Friday. Hazin is the reason they're so popular now!'

Flo knew all about where the rich and beautiful gathered.

Dion's was a bar set within a very plush hotel. It had once been a sedate place to gather for pre-theatre drinks and dinner.

It was old-fashioned and had become oddly trendy, a sort of retro fifties-style bar that people now lined up to get into.

'You could go there tonight and tell Hazin that you need to speak with his brother.'

'Just walk in and tap him on the shoulder?' Maggie rolled her eyes.

'Get talking.' Flo shrugged. 'Flirt a little...'

'I'm nearly six months pregnant by his brother!'

'Oh, yes, I see your point.'

'And I doubt Hazin would be particularly pleased to see me. I caused an awful lot of trouble for him. No doubt he thinks I was involved in the plan to set him up.'

Maggie had been unwittingly used in a plan to stitch up Hazin and bribe the Palace. She had ended up in Hazin's cabin aboard his Royal yacht where a camera had been hidden overhead.

But whoever had assumed that Maggie would drop her bikini bottom for Hazin had not known her.

Maggie and Hazin had done nothing but have a conversation.

Not that the Palace had known that at the time. Ilyas had kidnapped Maggie to find out what had happened aboard the yacht.

Yes, *kidnapped*, Flo reminded her friend. 'Which, in my opinion, means you're under no obligation to tell him.'

'I want to, though.' Maggie said. 'Flo, I know I've given you an awful impression of Ilyas but he really was wonderful to me.'

He must have been, Flo conceded, because Maggie trusted so few people.

Flo thought for a moment. She didn't want to go to Dion's, it was where she had met her ex and he still drank there on occasion.

Maggie didn't know about that; she'd had enough troubles of her own since she'd returned from Zayrinia, without Flo piling on hers.

That wasn't the full reason, though. Maggie and Flo were close and usually she would have told her, but the break-up that had happened last Christmas, when Maggie had been away, had hurt Flo deeply.

And Flo was still terribly ashamed.

No, she did not want to go to Dion's tonight.

In fact, Flo hadn't really had a night out since last Christmas.

Maggie's baby was due a week after this one.

She looked at her friend, who had no family and was pregnant and scared, and Flo put on her smile.

She was very good at doing that and keeping her thoughts to herself. 'I could always come with you to Dion's after my shift,' Flo offered.

And so it had been arranged.

'I have to go.' Flo glanced at the time. 'I'm going to be late.'

She was often late, though not usually for work. It tended to be the other way round—she would stay on at work and arrive late for her life.

Men didn't seem to like that, Flo had worked out.

At least, not the ones she was used to.

Flo's shift had been a good one.

She was a midwife on the maternity unit at the Primary Hospital in London. It was a busy, modern hospital but, as much as Flo loved it, sometimes she yearned for more one-on-one time.

She had been rostered to work in Delivery but had instead been moved to the ward. There she had caught up with a mother she had cared for in the delivery unit the previous day. It had been a difficult birth and had ended in an emergency Caesarean.

Tonight, at the end of her shift, Flo had held the outcome in her arms.

Rose.

'She looks like one.' Flo had smiled, for Rose was delicate and pink and utterly oblivious to the terrible scare she had given everyone.

'Thanks for all you did, Flo,' Claire, the mother, had said.

Flo had smiled as she'd looked down at the tiny baby. Very rapid decisions had needed to be made and the petite, fun-loving Flo had snapped into action and become extremely vocal.

In her private life she did not stand up enough for herself, but at work, when looking out for the mothers and babies, she was very different indeed.

Her job was exhausting.

Quite simply, it was always so busy and it was a constant juggling act to give enough attention to the mothers.

Tonight, though, she had a moment.

Several of them.

At twenty-nine, and with her ovaries loudly ticking, Flo would have loved a baby of her own. Still, she got more than a regular fix of that delicious newborn scent each working day. 'Your beautiful daughter has reminded me exactly why I love my job,' Flo said.

She popped the sleeping baby back into her Perspex crib and then reset Claire's IV.

'Are you on tomorrow?' Claire asked.

'No, but I'm back on Monday. You should be about ready for discharge then but I shall do my best to come in and see you both.'

She looked again at little Rose, so peaceful and safe, and then Flo turned at a knock on the door and saw it was her senior.

'Flo, it's time to give your handover.'

It was just after nine, and for the first time in a very long time it seemed that Flo might just get away on time.

She did.

Flo raced back to her flat and had a very quick shower. She was used to getting ready quickly to go out.

Or she had been.

Not all men were bad, Flo knew that.

She saw evidence every day that good guys existed. Her parents had just celebrated their thirtieth wedding anniversary and her brothers and sisters were all happily married. At work, she regularly saw fathers support their partners and she worked with an amazing team.

Yes, she knew there were good guys, but she had met the other kind too.

Flo grabbed a sheer, grey dress and high-heeled shoes and then quickly set to work on her hair and make-up.

She put her hair up and quickly did her eyes, followed by a slick of neutral colour on her lips. She was about to add earrings when her hands paused over her jewellery tray.

It was a testimony to her disastrous love life. Flo knew she had been too easily appeased by bling.

She had thought the more expensive the gift, the deeper the commitment.

Flo knew now she could not have been more wrong.

And so she left the earrings off and raced for the underground, firing Maggie a quick text on the way.

Ten minutes

It would be more like twenty, Flo knew, but she also knew Maggie would be terribly nervous and looking for an excuse to walk away.

Flo was more than a little concerned at the predicament her friend was in. Maggie had been raised in foster and care homes and had no family to advise her. As a midwife, Flo was well versed on single mothers who were facing difficulties alone. She wasn't exactly trained, though, in advising women who were pregnant by a future King.

Goodness!

She hurried up the escalator, came out of the underground and arrived out on the street a little breathless.

Even from that distance she could see the queue and wondered if there was even a hope of them getting in. She knew just how exclusive it was.

'Flo!'

Marcus, the doorman, called her name and Flo flashed her winning smile as she walked over, thrilled to be remembered. 'I'm just waiting for my friend to arrive.'

'Well, you could both be waiting for a very long time if you don't come in now,' Marcus told her. 'I'm being moved to security inside in a moment so there will be someone else on the door.'

Flo wavered and looked down the street, but there was no sign of Maggie.

'You can leave your friend's name at the front desk,' he suggested.

To the moans of the queue, the velvet rope was lifted and Flo was allowed in.

'You have to hand in your phone,' Marcus warned. 'So maybe text her now.'

'Why do I have to hand in my phone?'

'Orders from the top.'

Ah, so Hazin *must* be here.

His bad-boy ways had been captured on camera one too many times, Flo guessed, and the management would not want to upset him. She fired Maggie a quick text to meet inside, left her name at the desk and then made her way in.

Dion's was very beautiful. There were intimate velvet booths for diners, a gleaming walnut bar, and occasional tables where patrons could sip their cocktails and beverages of choice.

The place was packed with endless, rich beauty, and though it had once excited her, now it left Flo rather cold.

She had been caught up a little in this world once and, having been a lot more innocent back then, she'd believed that men had actually wanted to get to know her!

Instead, they had wanted her to hang quietly on their arm and not ask too many questions.

Yes, she'd been hurt.

Badly so.

But she pushed it to the back of her mind and squeezed her way over to the bar.

A couple looked as if they were about to vacate a table and Flo debated whether to grab it or to go and order first.

But then she saw him.

Sheikh Prince Hazin al-Razim.

He wore a suit that was as black and superbly cut as his hair. His tie was loosened and he was so stunning that he actually stopped Flo in her tracks.

How the hell did a person even begin to approach that? she pondered, thinking of her suggestion to Maggie to approach casually. And then she thought of Maggie alone in a cabin with him for two hours!

Had she been the one alone with him on a yacht, they would not have been talking!

Hazin was as utterly gorgeous as that.

He wasn't banned from bringing in his phone, of course.

In fact, he was checking it and Flo could tell he was getting ready to leave.

Indeed, Hazin was about to go.

He was supposed to have met his older brother an hour ago and hadn't been looking forward to it in the least. He did not need another lecture on taming his ways, but Ilyas had been insistent that they meet.

And then hadn't bothered to show.

They were not close. In fact, thanks to their upbringings, Hazin and Ilyas were practically strangers. They had been segregated as children and when Hazin had proven rather a handful he had been sent to be schooled in London.

Ilyas wore the robe in the relationship and Hazin the suit.

Ilyas would be King.

Hazin simply did not care for any of that and did all he could not to return home, for there was no welcome waiting, just lectures on his behaviour that had been on repeat from as far back as Hazin could remember. As well as that, he loathed how his father ran the country, for it was in the same way in which King Ahmed parented—no empathy and with disdain for those he was charged to care for.

To Hazin's eyes, Ilyas was as staid and cold as his father.

There was no message on his phone to explain his brother's lateness, and looking up Hazin glanced around the place.

He was sick of Dion's and the empty, painted people.

But then he saw her.

Or rather he heard the barman laugh at something and looked to its source.

She was ordering a glass of wine and a sparkling water and as she waited for her drinks she turned to look around. Her china-blue eyes met his.

'Hi,' she said.

He gave a very slight nod, but he didn't find her forwardness particularly fetching. She was gorgeous, that was a given, but Hazin was more than used to women making a move on him and the gloss had long since worn off.

Flo could sense his disinterest and that he was about to leave; she wondered what she should say and how best to introduce herself. She glanced towards the main door and wished Maggie would arrive, but there was no sign of her. 'I'm waiting for a friend.'

Hazin said nothing, for it had nothing to do with him.

'She's late,' Flo pushed.

Hazin accompanied his tight smile with a put-down. 'And I'm leaving.'

He had no interest in offering to keep her company. He was tired of being chatted up just for his Royal title and the empty sex that followed.

These days, he practically had to pat them down first to check for cameras anyway.

Then he watched as she stifled a yawn.

It was not the response Hazin was used to. Usually they hung on his every word.

Yes, he was jaded.

'Excuse me,' Flo said. 'I just came from work...'

She was tired and yet also energised in the magnetic presence of Hazin, and unsure whether to tell him who her friend was and that Maggie would soon be arriving, but then he asked a question.

'What do you do for work?'

'I'm a midwife.'

He pulled such a horrified face that it made her laugh.

And then Hazin became curious.

'I haven't seen you here before...' Hazin said, because he would have remembered if he had.

She wasn't just pretty, she was animated and a shade different from the rest, he thought.

'No, I used to come here quite a lot but I've banned myself,' Flo said, and took a sip of her wine.

'Why?'

'I'm not telling you.' She smiled.

Oh, hurry up, Maggie, she thought, because he was utterly, recklessly stunning and now that he was talking to her she could peek shamelessly without looking odd.

He had smoky grey eyes and his skin was a burnt caramel. As for his mouth, she couldn't not watch it when he spoke, and those plump lips needed to be kissed.

She should have gone out more, Flo thought, for she felt like a convent schoolgirl set free.

'Do you want to get a table?' Hazin offered, because all of a sudden he wasn't that jaded and was very much up for being used.

Well, a table would be perfect actually, Flo thought. It meant he wouldn't be leaving and Maggie would get here to find them both sitting and talking, like sensible adults.

Only right now Flo didn't want to be sensible, and she was suddenly nervous about going and sitting down.

There was a crackle of awareness between them, stronger than she had ever known.

'I doubt we'd get a table…' she said, terrified of her own lack of resistance to him, and then pulled a little face behind his back as he had a word with the bar.

'Done.'

But they didn't get a table.

Hazin and his glass of water were worthy of a booth.

He was so broad shouldered that the people parted like the Red Sea for him and she should have walked a smooth path behind, except her thighs felt like they were made of rubber.

'After you,' he said, and she slid into a velvet-lined seat and let out a tense breath of relief when he took the seat opposite, instead of sliding in beside her.

'I'm Hazin.'

She noticed he did not offer his title.

This man did not need a title to have her feeling weak from the waist down.

He thought that perhaps, if she hadn't been coming to Dion's for a while, she might not know who he was. It was a refreshing thought—to lose the burden of it for a night.

'You?' he asked.

'Flo,' she said. 'Florence.'

'Like that old nurse?'

'Florence Nightingale?' she checked, and he nodded. 'Well, she wasn't old in her day,' Flo corrected him. 'Do you perhaps mean that nurse from olden times?'

'I do.'

She smiled.

Hazin was well schooled but English was his second language and occasionally he slipped. Anyway, language and its intricacies could hardly be expected to be at the forefront of his mind when in the presence of such loveliness.

He liked her matter-of-fact correction that had come with a smile. Hazin had been raised to know any deviation from perfection would not be tolerated.

Yes he was wild, but whether it was a misspelt birthday card to his father, a torrid fling, or being born second in line, the verdict was always the same.

Not good enough.

So he no longer tried and instead happily disappointed everyone.

His sins would never be forgiven so Hazin had long since stopped apologising for them.

It made no difference when he did.

'So,' he asked, wanting to know more of her, 'why have you banned yourself?'

'Because the people here are terribly shallow.'

'Yes.'

'And my ex comes here…' Flo explained just a little.

'Were you hoping to see him?'

'God, no.' Flo grimaced at the very thought. 'I'm not just avoiding Dion's, I've been staying home a lot of late.'

'For how long?'

'All this year.'

'Why?'

'I'm off men.'

He looked at Flo and he wondered, in a way that was unusual for him, what on earth had happened that she would hide her light away.

'Why?'

'I don't want to talk about it.'

Flo hadn't told anyone.

Not a single soul.

Yet his eyes looked right into hers and his smile was non-judgmental and kind.

But, no, she would not be telling him.

'So are you off *all* men?'

She swallowed because just a short while ago her response would have been an unequivocal yes.

Except he was ravishing.

And funny.

But mainly he was ravishing.

His eyes weren't a uniform grey—this close she could see there were little flecks of green and amber.

'I think so.'

'Isn't it a bit extreme?' he asked. 'To hide yourself away…?'

'Perhaps,' Flo said. 'Yes.'

'Would you like another drink?' he offered.

'No, thank you.' She glanced at his empty glass. 'Can I get you one?'

She was frantic to get some control here—to go and

stand at the bar again so she could remind herself how to breathe, but Hazin would not let her get away that easily.

'I don't drink,' he said. 'I can have your friend's soda water. It doesn't look as if she's going to show.'

'No.'

She looked around the bar and wondered what to do. Perhaps Maggie had changed her mind about letting Ilyas know about the baby.

Flo felt a little lost without her phone.

And then she saw him.

Her ex.

The reason why she had been hiding for so long.

Bastard.

She flicked her eyes away from her past and back at Hazin.

At least this man didn't pretend he wasn't one.

'Are you okay?' Hazin asked, because he didn't usually lose his audience.

'My ex is here,' Flo said, and she held her breath as out of the corner of her eye she saw him make his way over.

Hazin watched her very pretty face pale rather than flush and he knew she'd been badly hurt.

And then he knew why.

Hazin was a regular here and had watched this creep pick up someone on one night and bring his wife for a meal the next.

Hazin might be wild now, but he had been married once and he'd taken his vows seriously, so, when it was clear from her panicked silence that she could not deal with her ex, Hazin was more than happy to.

'Flo's busy,' Hazin said in a surly tone. 'Please leave.'

'Now look here—' the man started, but then Hazin stood up.

'I did ask politely,' Hazin said and Flo could not believe there was about to be a fight.

What the hell?

He was more than up for a fight, but instead he gestured with his head for Marcus.

'I just want to speak to Flo,' the man insisted.

'Well, you can't,' Hazin said, 'because, as of now, you are barred from this establishment.'

It was Marcus's problem now because, as Flo's ex loudly protested as he was steered away, Hazin took his seat again. 'He shan't trouble you again,' Hazin said. 'At least, not when you're here.'

The shadow in the room was gone and she experienced the giddy feeling of some measure of retribution at last.

Now Flo examined him and no longer did she hide that fact.

And Hazin did the same.

She was used to the roaming of male eyes over her body but his eyes did not leave her face.

And yet his gaze was indecent.

He traced the curves of her lips with his eyes so thoroughly that Flo fought not to run her tongue over them.

It felt as if he studied each eyelash in turn until she silently pleaded for him to fully meet her gaze.

Then when he did it was fire versus fire.

Beneath the table, she could envision his spread knees for they seemed to encircle hers, which were pressed tightly together. She could feel their surrounding warmth and almost craved the tight pressure of his grip.

'I think I should go,' Flo said, because it was clear Maggie wasn't going to show.

'I can't hear you.'

Liar, liar, Flo thought as she gazed deep into his eyes, for here in the booth they were sequestered from the thrumming noise of the bar.

She could say it a little louder, reach for her purse and leave, or she could lean in a little closer to that delicious mouth and repeat what she had just said.

Or she could simply make the complicated so terribly easy.

Flo chose the latter—'Come and sit by me, then.'

No, she didn't want another drink, or conversation; she wanted this...

His kiss.

CHAPTER TWO

IT FELT AS if the oxygen masks had tumbled out on the plane, for even before he was seated she reached up for his tie and pulled him in.

The attraction had been instant, the effect close up magnetic, for they were so strongly drawn to each other that first contact offered Flo a heady feeling of relief. Hazin lowered his head and their mouths met before he was even fully seated. His lips were warm and Flo's pouted to his.

Soft and sensual, his mouth claimed hers as he slid into the booth beside her.

She had never known a kiss like it, for it sent a river of shivers through her and the brief bliss of relief faded for she *had* to taste his tongue, yet Hazin made her wait. His hands came to her upper arms and he held her steady when she ached to lean into him.

Still no tongue, just the bruising of his mouth and a breathless rush of desire in an outwardly chaste kiss. Then his mouth left hers and she felt its warm drag against her cheek and the scratch of his jaw as his lips found her ear. His breath was warm and he told her his truth. 'I want you so badly.'

His voice was so loaded with lust that it sounded as if he were already inside her.

Her sex clenched to his words.

She had no resolve.

None.

For a second she sat, his cheek pressed to hers, his ragged sexy breathing in her ear and his hands firm on her arms, and Flo closed her eyes in a vague prayer for common sense to prevail.

It didn't.

Fired on by one kiss, her body crackled like a chip in hot oil and she offered her response to his indecent request. 'Take me to bed.'

As soon as the night air hit her, sense would appear, Flo reassured herself as they stood. He took her by the hand and she was rather glad for the support as he led her through the bar.

But not to the street.

No cool air to hit her.

No car or taxi to calm her mind.

They were in an elevator. He hit the button and even that jab of his finger had her almost fold. And then that same finger stroked her nipple and she simply watched, entranced.

Was it her self-imposed ban on men that had her so frantic? Flo wondered. But, no, that wasn't right, for she had never felt like this in her life.

She was turned on to her very core. When he removed his hand she took it and pressed his palm to her face then deep-kissed his hand.

He moaned and said something in Arabic and then, when the elevator doors opened, Flo dropped his hand and they stood for a second facing each other.

She had to have his mouth.

Yet he just gave a slow smile and with an utter lack of haste he turned and walked down the long corridor.

For a hotel, there was a distinct lack of doors, Flo thought vaguely, for her mind was muddled by him.

They came to one, though, and he opened it. They stepped in and she realised the lack of doors was because his suite took up the entire floor.

A rainy London night glittered before them. Flo could see the Houses of Parliament, and Big Ben told her it was after midnight, yet the landmarks, so loved and familiar to her, were now altered in her mind. How could she ever gaze upon the time again and not remember the feel of him coming up behind her?

His hands dealt with her zipper and she just stood there as her dress fell to the floor.

She turned her head, needing his touch, for little slivers of doubt were raining in.

'Kiss me...' she said.

'Of course.'

But still he denied her the taste of his mouth for his lips went to her shoulder and he tasted her there as he slowly removed her bra.

'Hazin...'

'Do you mean, kiss you here?' he asked, and turned her around so he could kiss her breast.

Softly, slowly and indecently.

The doubt he'd sparked was intentional, Flo realised, and it now felt delicious. The hovering of uncertainty was dizzying as he kissed down her stomach.

Hazin removed her knickers and then he kissed her calves as he carefully slipped off her shoes.

'Sit down,' he told her.

'Where?'

'You choose.'

She couldn't.

Flo looked around at the stunning surroundings and

blinked in confusion. She was naked while he was fully dressed and she was actually trembling with desire.

'How about here?' Hazin suggested as he indicated one of the high-backed wooden chairs from a large polished dining table.

'It doesn't look very comfortable.'

'Poor Flo,' he said as he brought the chair over.

The wood was cold and hard on her bottom and she wasn't certain she liked this game, yet she complied willingly.

He was still completely dressed—he hadn't even removed his jacket—and the only concession to her nakedness was that he further loosened his tie.

'Are you going to spank me?' Flo asked, curious because she had never been spanked before. In fact, she would absolutely refuse it.

Not with him…

'Why would I spank you?' he asked. 'When you've been so good?'

'Oh.'

'I'm going to reward you.'

He knelt down and his hands parted her thighs. 'Hazin…' Flo objected. It was all too clinical. She didn't want flowers but, hell, a kiss would be nice.

And then he did kiss her.

But…*there*.

He just scooted her bottom out before lowering his head and thoroughly kissing her. He could be as clinical as he liked if it meant this! He moved her calves to rest on his broad shoulders as she hung onto the edge of the chair.

His tongue was insistent and he moaned with intent. It was so focused and thorough and Flo found that tears threatened. Her thighs were trembling but his arms clamped them down. She let go of the chair and buried her hands into his hair. His tongue grew more rapid in its intimate perusal and her bottom tried to lift as she began to climax, but he pinned her down and she tugged at his thick black hair as she met utter bliss.

Then he stood and simply picked her up and did as she had asked.

He took her to bed.

It was already turned down, but he pushed the sheets further back and deposited her there.

And she lay on her side, trying to recover and somewhat bemused as she watched him undress, for she had wanted to do that part.

Hazin was like no other lover.

He kicked off his shoes and peeled off his socks.

She wanted to feel the muscled arms beneath the white shirt.

Yet he denied her that pleasure.

She wanted to tug at his belt and to feel him, yet she breathlessly watched instead.

God, he was exquisite.

Lean and strong and completely unabashed. He smiled over to her, an arrogant smile, and she returned it, for they were feasting on each other with their eyes.

He went into the bedside drawer and took out a condom. She reached out to touch him but he slapped her hand back. Again she had to settle for watching and she bit on her lip as he stood and gave his long thick length a couple of deft strokes before sliding on the condom.

It shouldn't have been sexy, yet it absolutely was. She was burning from her roots to her toes, on fire as he climbed into bed beside her.

And then finally, *finally* he kissed her.

He rolled her onto her back and he gave her all that

had been denied until now. His tongue was probing and his mouth was urgent and rough. Finally, she felt those muscled arms and the satin of his skin. He drove into her and she cried out because he was not a gentle lover, but his controlled power was the just the right kind roughness, for he stroked her deep inside and seemed to read her wants instinctively.

Hazin spoke in Arabic, yet she somehow understood every word, for they *were* so hot together and so damned good.

Worries fell like dominos.

That row at work? Gone.

The bastard earlier? Forgotten.

Obsolete.

Hazin felt the same.

For the first time utterly attuned to another person.

He had tasted her first peak of pleasure, but the second gripped him and the shudder and pulsing grip of her just about finished him.

'Hazin,' Flo begged, because she was utterly spent, and then, when it should have been over, he kissed her back.

A kiss so soft and slow it tasted of the romance both had denied.

It was like finding herself in the wrong dream.

Scary almost to know him tender as well as urgent and passionate.

And even scarier for Flo to reveal her other side.

Flo opened her eyes and met his and there was a moment of utter connection. Her legs loosened their grip on him and he thrust slowly. So intimate and slow were they that she deep-kissed his neck, tasting the salt of his skin, as they locked into each other; tasting each other, and raining kisses as he took her to a place she had never been.

It felt like the edge of something, like she had finally stumbled into the right dream as he called her name and reached his own moment of release. And when there was nothing left to give, her body found an untapped resource, for she beat to his tune, this utter giddying orgasm, that only he could evoke.

His weight on her felt necessary and, oh, so right.

She could lie there and not think for a moment, just enjoy the bliss of them both sated.

He really was bliss, for there was no dark silence afterwards, just a light kiss and the warmth of his embrace.

'I'm glad you were there tonight,' Hazin said.

So was she.

Flo awoke, of course, with regret.

Please, she bargained with the powers that be, reverse this mistake and I will give up men for life.

Then she felt the wet of his tongue and the warmth of his breath on her neck and the light dusting of his fingers on her stomach.

And then the tearing of the condom foil lit her like a match as he pulled her against him.

Tomorrow, she vowed as he slipped inside her.

She would start being good tomorrow.

CHAPTER THREE

HAZIN SHOWERED AND thought of the woman who now lay in his bed.

He liked her being there.

Flo made him laugh and that in itself was unusual for there had been little laughter of late.

As a rule, Hazin offered no breakfast with bed that might encourage an overnight guest to stay longer, but he came out and dried himself with a towel and found he had not changed his mind—he wanted her here.

'Do you want breakfast?'

'That would be lovely,' Flo said, and sat up as he picked up the bedside phone and ordered breakfast for two.

She did not know how to tell Hazin that she knew who he was and wished that she had got it out of the way last night.

Now she stood watching him dry off. There was a bruise on his chest that her mouth had made and another on his neck. He was muscled and toned and his length was rising from his thigh. He watched her watching it.

'Did I miss a bit?' he said, holding the towel out to her. She wanted to take it, to dry his glistening skin and then wet him again with her mouth. Their want and desire was so matched, and her body so willing, but she had to clear things up first.

'Hazin,' Flo said, declining the towel, and she swallowed nervously as he resumed his leisurely drying off. 'Last night, I came—'

'I know.'

'I mean I came to Dion's in the hope...' Her words were coming out wrong, Flo knew that, but she just didn't know how best to tell him. So she simply did. 'I knew that you'd be here.'

The towel stopped in mid-stroke of his thigh.

'Meaning?' he said, and then gave a derisive laugh. 'You know who I am.'

'Yes, but—'

'Did you get your photo of me?'

'Hazin!'

'Or are you off to sell your story now?'

'Please listen—'

'No, you listen.' He pulled on his clothes with some difficulty for the angry words had fired him, and as he attempted to tuck himself in, words hissed out through his teeth. 'Do what you want. I don't care...'

'I'm a friend of Maggie's.'

'Who?'

'The woman you met on the yacht...'

'You mean the one who bribed me?'

'No.' Flo knelt up on the bed, shaking her head, and then she pulled the sheet up to cover her for everything had vanished in a heartbeat—the intimacy, the carefree nakedness, the laughter, all that they had so recently found swept away by her careless words.

'Hazin...' She took a breath, and though her mouth was open she did not know what to say.

Clearly Maggie had stayed away last night for a reason. Perhaps she had changed her mind about telling Ilyas that she was carrying his child?

And now certainly wasn't the time or place to tell Hazin!

'Get out,' he said, and his voice whipped the tense air.

'Hazin, what happened last night had nothing to do with Maggie. I didn't come to the bar intending to sleep with you.'

He was too used to this, Hazin thought as he marched through to the lounge and retrieved her underwear and dress that they had so happily disposed of last night. He walked back to the bedroom and tossed them to her on the bed.

'Get out!' he said again.

But then he changed his mind, for he could not wait however long it would take her to dress for Flo to be gone. 'Actually, I'm going to go,' he told her. 'I want you out of here by the time I get back. If you're not, I'll ask Security to have you removed.'

She knew how effective his security was.

He grabbed his wallet and phone and pocketed his keys.

'Stay for breakfast at least,' he sneered. 'You certainly earned it.'

Hazin kicked at the kerb as he walked down the street.

It was grey, raining and cold.

His phone kept ringing and he was in no mood to talk to anyone. It couldn't be Flo because they hadn't exchanged numbers yet pulled it out to check.

It was Ilyas.

Ilyas was persistent and Hazin was in just the mood for a row.

'What the hell happened to you last night?' Hazin shouted by way of greeting when he took the call.

'We need to speak.'

'Well, had you turned up as arranged we would have.'

'Hazin, this is important.'

They met at a café and drank strong coffee.

Hazin could feel his brother's eyes sweep over his neck and the bite mark Flo had left. 'I don't need another lecture.'

'I'm not here to lecture you,' Ilyas said.

'And I don't need to be reminded that the yachts and jets will be pulled. I can afford to pay for my own.'

Hazin was not idle.

After Petra's death he had returned to England with the intention to further his education and attend university, as had always been his aim. He hadn't been able to focus, though, so had started to dabble in property.

Whatever Hazin dabbled in did well.

He did not need Royal privilege to survive; in fact, without it Hazin thrived. Yes, he had been given an amazing start but he had a good eye and even if he had been born to a beggar he still would have done well.

His parents knew it and loathed that fact.

'Hazin,' Ilyas said, 'I have already told you that I am not here to lecture you. I have something important to tell you—yesterday I spoke with our father in front of the Palace elders and I told him that things are changing—'

'They will never change.' Hazin dismissed the notion. 'Not while he is King.'

'I have told him that there are to be no decisions made without my approval and that there is to be a transition of power to me.'

Now Hazin looked up. 'He would never agree to that.'

'I gave him no choice but to agree. I made it clear that if he refused then I am prepared to take it to the people,' Ilyas said. 'Would I have your support?'

'You don't need it.'

'I want it, though.'

Hazin looked at his brother.

A stranger.

He wanted to believe change could happen, yet could not really see it taking place. Yet there was a stir of relief within Hazin that his brother would be stepping up, an intrinsic trust that Ilyas would get things right, yet he did not know where that feeling came from for they had been raised apart. 'You have my support.'

'I want you beside me.'

'Oh, no.' Hazin shook his head. He would support his brother in his ventures but he would not be returning home.

'Hazin, there has been a lot of damage done by him. If things are to be put right it's going to take a lot of work to win back people's trust. You returning to Zayrinia would speak volumes.'

'You expect me to upend my life on the premise that things *may* change?'

'They shall change. And there is something else I am here to tell you,' Ilyas said. 'I am going to marry in two weeks' time.'

'So much for change.' Hazin shrugged and took a drink of his coffee. Ilyas had always refused to marry, insisting the harem more than sufficed. 'You simply gave in to him.'

It had infuriated their father that Ilyas had refused to marry. He had long wanted to select a bride for his son and for there to be a Royal wedding.

At the age of eighteen Hazin had received his exam results. He had worked incredibly hard and the results had been outstanding.

His father hadn't even commented.

Instead of attending university in England, as had been Hazin's dream, finally he'd found something he could do that might please his father the King.

There was going to be a Royal wedding—Hazin's.

Petra had been chosen as his bride and they had first met at the wedding itself.

Both had been eighteen and Hazin could well remember looking out from the balcony at the cheering crowds and wondering what the hell he had done, while trying to hide it from his bride.

Ilyas dragged him from his introspection. 'You remember Maggie?'

Hazin frowned at the sound of that name again.

He hadn't seen her in six months. Even then, all they had shared was a conversation and that alone had caused so much trouble.

Yet in the space of an hour he had heard her name twice.

Once from Flo, now from his brother.

'What about her?'

'Last night I asked Maggie to marry me.'

Hazin suddenly felt caught.

Nothing at all had happened between Maggie and himself. It had been a set-up and the cameras watching had hoped something would.

It hadn't.

But Hazin had asked the Palace to pay the ransom demand because of the conversation that had taken place between them. Thankfully, though, their voices had not been recorded and so no one other than Maggie knew what had been said.

He had spoken openly, perhaps far too openly, but he had felt safe in the knowledge he would never see Maggie again.

Yet now he was being told she was to marry his brother!

Had she told Ilyas what he had said?

'Maggie is pregnant,' Ilyas told him. 'The baby is due in three months.'

'So while you were nailing me to the wall for something Maggie and I didn't do, all the time you were—'

'Hazin,' Ilyas interrupted, 'I had Maggie brought to the desert to find out what was going on, because I assumed she was blackmailing you. She wasn't. We fell in love.'

And that silenced Hazin, for it was something he'd never thought he would hear from Ilyas's mouth.

His brother had always seemed cold and aloof and yet he was sitting in a café, telling him there would be changes in the Palace and that he had fallen in love.

And, yes, Maggie had spoken.

The content of the conversation had been private. Words had been said to a stranger with confidence they would never meet again.

Instead, Ilyas relayed what he had said that day.

'Maggie told me you said on the yacht that you hoped to be disinherited.'

'Well, she shouldn't have repeated what was clearly a private conversation,'

'It remains just between us. I shall not be taking what was said to the elders.'

Oh, Ilyas was so controlled and formal, Hazin thought, and shot him a look as he spoke on.

'I understand too that you don't want to speak at Petra's anniversary…'

'Maggie's been busy!' Hazin sneered.

'I had to drag the conversation from her.'

Hazin felt as if his most private thoughts were being raked over by a stranger.

'I know this must be difficult for you,' Ilyas attempted. 'You must miss Petra—'

He knew *nothing*.

Ilyas, who had always been so distant, suddenly reaching out did not sit right with Hazin.

'We don't talk, Ilyas. We never have, unless it was you telling me to raise my game. You know nothing of my life yet ten years after Petra's death you sit here and tell me you know how I feel?' Hazin shook his head. 'Too late.'

'No.' Ilyas said. 'I want—'

'You can keep wanting, then,' Hazin said. 'But I have no desire to come back home, and certainly not for a wedding.'

The last one he had been to had been his own.

They had all assumed he had been blinded with grief since Petra's death and that was why he had gone off the rails.

They didn't know him at all and it was too late now to try.

'Why didn't you show up last night?' Hazin asked.

He saw Ilyas's slight eyebrow rise at the odd question, given the rather vital news, but Hazin was starting to realise what might have occurred.

'I went to see Maggie,' he said. 'She was actually on her way to try and meet you, so you could have me contact her.'

Hazin pressed his fingers into his forehead and closed his eyes. He could see now what had happened. Worse, he could see himself tossing Flo her clothes and shouting at her to get out.

He had to get back and try to explain somehow, and now had no desire to play catch-up with his brother.

'Good luck with the wedding,' Hazin said, and stood.

Ilyas did not try to dissuade him from leaving. They may not have been close, but he knew his younger brother would take time later to think it through.

And Hazin would.

Right now there was somewhere else he needed to be.

He walked briskly back to the hotel and took the elevator up to his floor. He pulled out his card and swiped the door open.

Too late.

Flo was gone.

He had known that she would be.

Hazin really hadn't imagined he'd find her sitting there, tucking into breakfast. Instead it had been set up on the table and remained untouched.

He walked through to the bedroom and the unmade bed.

There was the towel he had dropped on the floor and there was another so he guessed she must have showered and left.

Hazin walked back to the untouched breakfast and

felt a curl of guilt when he saw a box of tissues by the window and a little pile of knotted ones.

She'd been crying.

Hazin was very used to being a deliberate bastard.

This morning he'd been an inadvertent one.

CHAPTER FOUR

IF EVER THERE was a walk of shame, this was one. Not only was Flo clearly wearing last night's clothes, she'd also had to go down to the bar to retrieve her phone.

When she stepped out onto the street it was raining.

Of course it was, Flo thought as she trudged in high heels towards the underground.

What on earth had she been thinking last night?

Only she hadn't been thinking—one look into those smoky eyes and she'd forgotten why she was even at Dion's. How the hell was she going to tell Maggie the mess she had made of things?

And where the hell was Maggie?

Flo turned on her phone and on a cold, miserable wet morning there was suddenly a reason to smile.

Ilyas had proposed.

Oh, she was going to start crying again and hadn't thought to stuff her purse with tissues from the hotel.

So she used the back of her hand and read on and saw that Maggie wanted her to come straight over.

Er, that would be a no.

Flo first went back to her tiny flat and pulled on something a bit less *last night*!

Then she did what she could with foundation because

her chin was a little red and her mouth was all swollen from his delicious kisses and soft nips with his teeth.

She was going to start crying again, but that would not do.

So, instead of weeping, Flo headed over to her friend's and bought a bunch of flowers on the way.

'What happened?' Flo smiled, putting her own woes aside to celebrate the wonderful news with her friend, though there were rather too many stars in Maggie's eyes to see the threat of tears in Flo's.

'A lot,' Maggie said. 'I was just on my way to meet you when Ilyas came to the door. I'm so sorry I left you waiting…'

'Of course you did!' Flo said, for she totally understood the wonderful surprise that it must have been. 'What did he say about the baby?'

'He's thrilled,' Maggie said, but then her face became worried. 'I don't know how the people will react, though, or his family. Flo, there is so much going on back in Zayrinia—Ilyas has challenged his father, the King.'

'What does that even mean?'

'That Ilyas is to be the silent leader. From now on nothing is to get passed without his approval. He has told his father that if he doesn't comply then he will take it to the people.'

'What does that mean for you?'

'I'm not sure. I know that there's unrest amongst the people and that there has been a lot of unhappiness at the Palace. Ilyas wants change. He's gone to speak with his brother to see if he has his backing.'

Flo held her breath. She doubted she'd be at the forefront of Hazin's thoughts when he found out his brother was challenging the King, yet there was a tiny dart of hope that Hazin would maybe understand that she hadn't been at Dion's last night to seduce him.

Maggie had more news as well. 'After Ilyas has spoken with Hazin he's heading back to Zayrinia. Now that I've accepted his proposal I'm not allowed to see him until we marry.'

'At all?' Flo checked, and Maggie nodded. 'So when will you marry?'

'Two weeks' time!'

'Oh, my!' Flo looked at her friend and asked, perhaps, a stupid question, but it was all too much to take in. 'You'll live in Zayrinia?'

Maggie nodded. 'I'll still see you, though.'

Yes, Flo thought, but it won't be the same. She looked around Maggie's room within a flat, which she had helped her move into not long ago. She was thrilled for her friend but at the same time Flo was daunted by the distance. Maggie felt more like a sister than a friend. Flo stopped by the café where Maggie worked most days for a catch-up. She had a drawer full of clothes and necessities that she'd been buying for the baby.

And now both Maggie and the baby were moving away—in two weeks' time!

'I'm going to miss you,' Flo admitted.

'I won't give you a chance to. But, Flo, I'm so scared it will all go wrong. What if his father doesn't accept his choice of bride? This challenge to the King is so new and it was made before he knew about the baby. Ilyas knows that nothing happened between Hazin and me on the yacht but what if his parents don't believe us?'

'Maggie…' Flo attempted to calm her friend but Maggie was a touch frantic.

'I just don't want anything to go wrong.'

'It won't,' Flo said assuredly, deciding that now possibly wasn't the best time to tell Maggie she had just come from Hazin's bed! Maybe once the wedding was over and done with she would tell her friend what had happened last night.

But maybe not!

'You will come to the wedding?' Maggie checked.

'Of course I'll be there,' Flo said as she mentally stared down the eye of the off-duty roster. She had fought hard to have three weeks off at Christmas. It would be her first Christmas off since she had started nursing, but she would forfeit it if meant she could be there for her friend. 'I'll call work now.' Flo said. 'I'll see if I can swap some annual leave.'

Yet she didn't have to!

She and Maggie would arrive two days before the wedding and, Flo was delighted to find out, they would be flying in on Ilyas's plane.

And, given Maggie and Ilyas would be off to the desert straight afterwards, she didn't need much time off work.

It just meant a jiggle of the roster and Flo got to keep her Christmas leave.

Of course, while organising her leave there was a coil of hope rising that she would get to see Hazin!

It was the busiest run-up to a wedding and was beyond exciting.

Maggie sorted out her life and planned her big move, and Flo worked right up to the last minute.

'I am so tired,' she admitted, as she and Maggie, along with a couple of other good friends—Paul the café manager and his wife Kelly—all collapsed on the sumptuous leather seats on Ilyas's private jet. 'But not too tired for champagne!'

It was brilliant.

A whirlwind.

The take-off was abrupt and then they were served a sumptuous lunch of dips and then a delectable *kuku sabzi*—a Persian herb frittata with walnuts, decorated with crushed rose petals and berberis leaves, all washed down with a sweet hibiscus tea.

Paul and Kelly went for a rest in one of the guest cabins but Flo refused hers; instead, she and Maggie went into the Royal suite.

'Oh, my gosh!' Flo said. 'You and Ilyas get to have sex here!'

There was a huge bed draped in furs, and the lighting was demure. It was just a sexy man cave miles in the sky. 'Is this just for Ilyas?' Flo asked, fishing a little.

'It is.' Maggie nodded.

'What about his parents?'

'They have their own plane.'

'And the brother?' Flo, oh, so casually asked.

'Hazin has his own, I believe,' Maggie said. 'They do their own thing.'

They lay on the bed together and marvelled at the journey ahead, as well as the one that had brought them here.

It was so nice to take some time out, for they simply had not had a chance to just relax and talk.

'What will happen about your antenatal care?' Flo asked.

'I'll have the Palace doctor apparently.'

'What about scans and things?'

'Anything I need shall be brought to the Palace but if there's a problem in labour and I need to go to the hospital there'll be a helicopter on standby.' She must have seen the dart of concern in Flo's eyes for Maggie spoke on. 'It's a ten-minute flight away. I don't think they'll be taking any chances with the future King.'

'Of course not.' Flo agreed, and then sighed. 'I'd have loved to deliver you.'

'Well, I know it's your job and everything but I'd find that strange.' Maggie smiled. 'A doctor that I rarely have to see suits me just fine.'

They decided to get some sleep so they put on the eye masks provided and lay there, drifting off. Flo wasn't offended in the least at Maggie's dismissal of her suggestion to deliver her. It was a moot point now anyway, given that she would be living so far away. Flo just knew how things changed when you were actually in labour. Maggie had no family. Well, of course she now had Ilyas, but when Flo had first offered, it had been because Maggie really had no one else.

She had Ilyas now, Flo consoled herself. And as Maggie herself had said, they were hardly going to take any risks with the future King.

It was her friend who concerned her, though.

'Hey, Flo…' Maggie said, as they lay in the dark, and the question that Flo had been anxiously avoiding, while simultaneously waiting for Maggie to ask, arose.

'Did you ever catch up with Hazin?'

'Sorry?' Flo pretended that she'd misheard.

'At Dion's, when you went there that night, did you speak to Hazin?'

'Is he going to be the best man?' Flo asked, terribly glad of the eye masks to cover her obvious change of subject.

'I don't think they have best men,' Maggie said. 'Anyway, he's not coming to the wedding apparently.'

'Not coming?' Flo frowned, whipping off her mask and sitting up. 'But he's Ilyas's brother.'

'I know that.' Maggie yawned. 'I hope he changes his mind.'

'Are they arguing?' Flo asked. 'Is that why he's not coming?'

'They don't talk enough to argue,' Maggie said. 'But I don't think it's that that's keeping Hazin away, I think it's more…'

'What?' Flo prompted, tempted to whisk off Maggie's eye mask and shake her for more information. But she held back from doing that and just hovered over her unseen.

'Hazin's wife died,' Maggie said. 'It's coming up for the tenth anniversary of her death and Hazin's dreading it apparently. They're opening a new oncology wing in her name. I think he still misses his wife and that's why he hates going back so much.'

Oh.

'How long were they married?'

'A year, I think,' Maggie said. 'They were very young.'

Flo sank back on the bed and lay there, listening to the hum of the engines, and she thought of Hazin and his lovely eyes and smile and the pain that must be behind them.

She could not get him out of her mind.

Despite working right up to the last minute, despite helping Maggie with all the wedding plans, she had not forgotten, even for a moment, the bliss of that night.

There should have been a stab of relief that there was now little chance of Maggie finding out before the wedding that she had slept with Hazin.

There wasn't, though.

Flo had been desperately hoping to see him, knowing that surely by now he would have worked out that she had been there about Maggie and not simply for a hook-up with a royal prince.

Perhaps he didn't care enough to work it out, Flo thought as she lay there.

She did, though.

She cared, not just what he thought of her but Flo had found that she cared for him.

The Rebel Prince.

A widower.

And also a man who would decide not to attend his own brother's wedding.

There was so much she wanted to find out and also to explain.

But if Hazin wouldn't be attending the wedding, there would be no chance to. None at all.

CHAPTER FIVE

The Palace was incredible.

Maggie had told her just how amazing it was but nothing could have properly prepared Flo for its splendour. The plane came in over the sea and Flo got her first glimpse of the stunning white building, a stark contrast to the burnt orange canyon it sat atop.

And, because they were aboard the Royal jet, they would land at the Palace. It was both terrifying and exhilarating as the plane aligned with the canyon. 'How big is this place?' Flo asked, still unable to fathom that it had its own landing strip.

'Huge,' Maggie said. 'And magnificent.'

They landed and were met by a woman named Kumu, who greeted them warmly, and they were then driven to a side entrance.

'The grand entrance,' Kumu explained, 'is used only by the Royals and for official occasions.'

And Maggie wasn't quite that yet, though the side entrance wasn't exactly shabby! They were led into a huge marble foyer and introduced to the wedding co-ordinator, who told them where they would be sleeping.

'Maggie, you asked to stay in the westerly wing in your previous suite and that has been accommodated.

The Palace is very full, though, with wedding guests arriving so your friends are in another section.'

It would seem that the westerly wing was rather *the* place to be, but Flo was just so thrilled to be here she really didn't care where she had been put.

Paul and Kelly were led off. 'Miss Andrews, I shall take you to your suite now and—'

'I'll go with Flo,' Maggie said. 'I want to know where she is.'

They were led through long corridors and up ancient steps and finally they arrived at what would be her home for the next few nights.

It was stunning.

The beautiful suite was bigger than her entire flat and the centrepiece was a high four-poster bed that was draped with heavy gold silk.

'There is no direct *hammam* access from here,' the co-ordinator regretfully explained.

'That's fine,' Maggie said. 'There's access from my suite so we can go from there.'

'Of course,' the co-ordinator agreed, 'but you cannot wander, Maggie. It is imperative that you do not see the groom, so when you are out of your suite, Kumu or I shall escort you.' Maggie was handed a schedule and when the co-ordinator had gone she and Flo went through it.

Basically, it was two days of utter bliss.

There was to be a lot of *hammam* time and a cleansing diet of fruit, then an hour from now the dressmaker would come to Maggie's suite to make adjustments.

'Dressmakers,' Flo corrected as she read through it. 'Oh, it's like a luxury retreat.'

'With a wedding at the end of it,' Maggie said, and Flo could hear the nervousness in her voice.

'It's going to be wonderful.'

'I know it is.' Maggie nodded. 'I just hate it that I can't see Ilyas until then. It feels like him coming to the flat was all a bit of a dream.'

'Well, it clearly wasn't,' Flo said, and she opened the huge French window. They stepped out onto the balcony to breathe the fragrant evening air.

'You have to come to my suite and see the sunset,' Maggie said. 'You've got planes for a view.'

'I like planes,' Flo said.

She actually did.

As Maggie went off for her fitting it was incredible to watch the private jets come in over the desert and see the helicopters land.

Dignitaries descended the steps of private jets in richly coloured robes. Some were taken by car while others walked across a small ornate bridge. It took an evening of sipping fragrant tea and eating slivers of fruit for Flo to work out that the more esteemed guests crossed the bridge rather than being met by a car.

Maggie clearly wasn't royal yet!

In the two days prior to the wedding, the bride-to-be and her guests were pampered and spoiled. There was a huge *hammam* beneath the Palace and because Paul and Kelly were married they were taken to the couples' area. Due to her impending status, Maggie had her own private section and Flo was allowed along for company.

'Think of it as one of our spa days,' Maggie had said the first time they had gone down there.

More often than not they gave each other a spa day for birthday presents. This meant that twice a year they got a wonderful girly day.

They weren't like this, though.

Their spa days had been taken in a swish hotel and

had always felt decadent as they lay wrapped in fluffy towels with face packs on, followed by a dip in a gorgeous pool.

Here, though, they were underground and they walked through tunnels decorated in mosaics. It really was another world. There were natural steam rooms and waterfalls and maids who took care of everything.

Maggie's long red curls were oiled in preparation for the big day and Flo's blonde hair received several treatments. Her skin was pummelled with salt, and by the time it came to Maggie's wedding day, all that was left to do was relax and prepare for the service, which was just a few hours away.

Maggie was nervous and Flo didn't blame her a bit. She hadn't seen Ilyas since he had proposed to her! Apparently his family was being difficult as Ilyas enforced the new order. Hazin was still a no-show, though his jet was apparently in Dubai. Yes, there was a lot for Maggie to be tense about. Not just the service—afterwards she would go out onto the balcony and the people would get their first glimpse of the obviously pregnant bride.

'It's going to be wonderful, Maggie,' Flo said as they lay being massaged, but despite her brave words even Flo could not let go of her tension.

Not just about the no-show of Hazin.

Today her best friend would be married and become a princess and the future Queen.

Flo looked over and, given she was so pregnant, Maggie lay on her back. Her eyes were closed as one maid massaged her scalp. Two others worked quietly on her feet.

No, it was not a regular spa day.

Flo was scared of change and did not want this valued friendship to slip away, yet she did not see how it could possibly stay the same.

She said nothing, though, for today was about the wedding, and Maggie was already nervous enough.

'What happens now?' Flo asked as they were led, wrapped in *hammam* towels, back through the tunnels to Maggie's suite.

'I guess hair and make-up,' Maggie said. 'I'll ask Kumu to have your clothes and things brought over to my suite.'

But it was not to be, for they found out that Flo could not be with Maggie in the final preparations.

'Only family can be present,' Kumu, who took care of details, explained.

'But Maggie doesn't have any family,' Flo said. 'I'm her closest friend. We're like sisters.'

'There can be no exceptions,' Kumu responded, and then turned to the bride-to-be. 'I am sorry, Maggie.'

'Surely…' Flo started, and was about to put on her assertive midwife voice, but she knew it might be best not to use it today so she changed her tone and turned to her friend. 'Maggie?' she checked. 'What do you want me to do?'

'I'll be fine,' Maggie said, but Flo could see that her teeth were chattering. 'You go and get ready.'

'In a bit,' Flo started, but it was clear she was no longer welcome.

'I'll see you at the service.' Maggie tried to be brave. 'Wish me luck.'

'You don't need luck,' Flo said. 'You're going to do beautifully. I just know it.'

Flo was not best pleased as she made her way to her suite, but there was nothing she could do.

The next time she saw Maggie it would be at the ceremony.

After that, Maggie and Ilyas and other Royals would appear on the Palace balcony and then there was to be a formal meal before the couple went to the desert.

She doubted there would be even a moment to speak properly with her friend.

And tomorrow Flo flew home to London.

Things were changing and there was nothing she could do, except get herself ready for the wedding.

Her hair had never been silkier and Flo decided she would leave it down, so she took out her tongs and added a few curls.

Then a few more.

Whatever oil they had used was amazing.

The treatments had done wonders for her skin and all she needed was a little blush and eyeliner and then mascara and she was done.

Flo put on a silk robe that had been left out for her and headed out onto the balcony, willing herself to be calm. Yet the sight of all the planes and helicopters was daunting. This was a huge Royal wedding and Maggie was facing it alone.

And as for Hazin…

She scanned the tails of the jets but she didn't know what she was looking for.

Flo just wanted to see him.

Not for the sake of his brother.

It was selfish of her perhaps, but she had an aching need to see Hazin again.

She and Maggie had been shopping before they'd left for Zayrinia and Flo had found the perfect dress.

It was full length and worked with all the guidelines, but it was bright red and as sexy as hell.

And had been bought with Hazin in mind.

She put on her very red lipstick, which had been bought with *both* the dress and Hazin in mind!

It killed her that he wouldn't be there to see it.

Surely he might still come, Flo thought as she headed to take her place in the gardens.

There was still no sign of Hazin, so the dress and lipstick were rather in vain.

But then she forgot about him when Maggie arrived.

She was smiling so widely and seemed utterly relaxed, so unlike the tense woman Flo had left.

It was the most beautiful ceremony, and it was clear they were deeply in love.

And there *was* time to speak after.

Maggie made the time for them.

'Did they drug you?' Flo beamed. 'You looked so calm…'

'Stop it.' Maggie laughed. 'Ilyas and I spoke before the ceremony.'

'You saw him?'

'No.' Maggie shook her head. 'We just spoke and it calmed me down a lot. I have to go out to the balcony now. Will you come up and wait for me there?'

'Of course.'

Ilyas and Maggie led the way back to the Palace and the Royals and Flo walked behind.

She wouldn't be going onto the balcony, of course, it was just nice to be a part of things. But then, just as they turned on the grand stairs, the entrance doors to the Palace opened and a sight for sore eyes staggered in.

Hazin.

His hair was dishevelled, and he was dressed in a crumpled suit and carrying a bottle of cognac. He clearly hadn't shaved in days.

'Keep walking,' someone advised, but of course the procession halted while Ilyas took charge and went to deal with his errant younger brother.

'Ilyas!' The Queen called him back but he ignored her summons. 'You...' the Queen said, and Flo was startled as she met the Royal glare. 'You're a nurse—deal with Hazin.'

'I'm a midwife, actually.'

'It's the same thing.' The Queen dismissed Flo with a wave of her hand.

Flo would have loved to tap her on the shoulder and correct her, but she had actually done her general nursing too.

It had been a very long time since she had been in the emergency department and dealing with drunks, though.

It was like riding a bike once you got down to it.

Hazin was led off by the guards and on the Queen's instructions Flo followed.

Down corridor after corridor they went and she found herself in an apartment within the Palace.

There the guards placed him on the bed.

'Thank you.' Flo smiled at them and when they were gone she stood there and looked at Hazin.

He really was terribly gorgeous with his tie undone and his shirt untucked. His eyelashes were flickering and she knew he was only pretending to be asleep. She looked at the bottle of cognac in his hand.

'I'm surprised you didn't drop it,' Flo said, and took it from his grip.

Yes, it *was* like riding a bike, for her training was ingrained and she knew he wasn't drunk!

Drunks weren't so pretty!

And Hazin had told her himself that he didn't drink.

'I know you,' he said as he opened one eye slightly.

'Indeed you do.'

She bent over and he frowned as her lips hovered over his.

'Is that within your nursy duties, Florence?'

'You're stone cold sober, Hazin. Couldn't you at least have taken a swig from the bottle?'

He smiled.

Busted.

'I can't stand the stuff.'

'Why didn't you just stay away if you didn't want to come?

Hazin didn't answer that.

It was a good question indeed.

'Why didn't you want to be at your brother's wedding?'

'It isn't the wedding so much…' He closed his eyes and it was all too hard to explain. 'Maybe it is,' Hazin said. 'The last wedding I was at…'

'Was yours.' Flo said. 'Maggie told me.'

'What else did she tell you?'

It was time to be honest, Flo decided, for pretending she had no idea who he was hadn't served them well. 'That you hope to be disinherited.'

'I never meant that to get out,' Hazin said, and he told her first-hand what had happened in his cabin that day. 'I was fed up,' he said. 'I had tried coming home for a visit but ended up taking out the yacht. I invited a few friends and…' He shrugged. It had been the usual debauched party. 'I was just tired of it and I went into my cabin and Maggie was there. She'd gone to lie down. I could tell she was upset and she mentioned it was the anniversary of her mother's death. She said how she missed having a family. I told her she was lucky, how

I was sick of mine, and that I wouldn't mind being dis-inherited. It was how I felt on the day. I might have no choice in the matter now.'

He was making the choice for them, Flo was sure, and she was rather sure she knew why. 'Maggie also said that you have to give a speech for the anniversary of your wife's death.'

'Ah, yes.'

He sank back on the pillows.

'When is that?'

'December.'

'It would be hard to do...'

'You have no idea,' he said, though not unkindly, more wearily. 'Go,' Hazin said after a little while. 'I don't need a nurse.'

'Could you use a friend?'

'I don't need one of those either.'

'Are you sure you want me to go?' Flo checked, and he nodded.

Hazin liked it that she didn't push and he watched her depart and close the door.

It felt odd, having her here.

Hazin behaved badly, but never when he was at home.

Not in this bedroom.

There had been no one since Petra in this bed.

The Palace and furnishings were intricate and an-cient. Hazin could hardly have a clear-out and pop out to the furniture store, so he had asked for a new suite in the Palace.

His father had told him to toughen up.

Hazin could tell no one his feelings.

He looked out at the glorious sky and wished the drapes were closed.

Everyone assumed they knew why he had gone off the rails—Hazin's grieving, they'd said.

Of course he had been grieving, for Petra had been nineteen when she'd died and he had done everything he could to save her. Flying in different doctors for opinion after opinion. An operation had left her unable to have children and he would never forgive his parents for their reaction to that news.

They felt they had chosen unwisely.

Hazin could not forgive them for that.

He had been by Petra's side every step of the way and had held her hand through the hell of surgery and chemotherapy. And, when there had been nothing more that could be done, Petra had asked to come home.

Here.

Her parents and brother had moved into the vast apartment and they had done all they could to love and support Petra.

Sometimes when tears had refused to remain hidden, Kumu, Petra's assistant, had stepped in and read to her or sat a while.

Hazin and his in-laws would step out onto the balcony and comfort and draw strength from each other before heading back to her side.

Now and then, Hazin would carry her from the bed to glimpse the desert and enjoy the warm breeze on her skin. Hazin had made her smile as often as he could. In fact, making Petra smile had been his daily mission.

But for all Hazin had cared, he hadn't loved Petra.

On his wedding day, staring out at the cheering masses, he'd known he had married in an attempt to please his father, rather than follow his dream and study classical archaeology and ancient history at university.

He had told Petra how much he loved her, though,

and had done everything he could not to let her know his truth.

Yet she had.

Right near the end of her far too short life, he had lain with her on this very bed, holding her to him, refusing to believe it was close to goodbye.

And then she'd said it. 'I want you to find true love, Hazin.'

'I have already found it.'

'No, Hazin. You have been a wonderful husband. I have been so happy in my time with you but I know you don't love me.'

'Petra—'

'Stop.' She had told him and he'd been able to see her struggle to open her eyes and that every breath had been an effort. 'I want you to find the one who makes your heart beat too fast.'

And then hers had stopped.

He loathed it that she had felt unloved.

To Hazin's eyes he had even messed up on Petra's deathbed.

CHAPTER SIX

FLO HEADED BACK down to the wedding celebrations, which were in full swing.

The feast was incredible and Maggie and Ilyas looked so happy. It was a wonderful occasion and full of food and much dancing.

And then came the gorgeous candle dance. Flo had no idea what it was but smiled as Maggie stood with two lit candles, just enjoying the goings-on, when unexpectedly she was handed one herself.

All the woman were, and with candles lit they stood behind the bride and followed her to the sounds of a soulful song. And then Flo was moved along the entourage so she stood by her friend and Flo realised then that this should have been Maggie's mum.

It was a special moment and Flo danced alone with her friend, who had been through so much.

And then it was the men's turn to dance and Maggie must have been thinking the same thing—that Hazin should be here.

Yet Flo understood why he could not be.

'How's Hazin?' Maggie asked.

'He'll be fine,' Flo said, but she didn't divulge to Maggie that he hadn't been drunk at all. 'I'll check on him later.'

As the celebrations eased down, and the bride and groom were about to leave for the desert, she said goodbye to her friend.

'Thank you for coming all this way.'

'It was hardly a burden. I've had the most wonderful time.'

And now it was goodbye.

Flo held back from crying until she could be alone in her suite. But she would miss Maggie terribly. They had been friends for years. When Flo had first started at the Primary she had found the chocolate café and their friendship had soon formed.

And she didn't know how this marriage and Maggie's new title might change that, only that she knew it would.

She was so ready for a good old howl that she actually forgot about Hazin, right up until she got to her suite.

His apartment was quite a walk from hers but she trudged down there.

Yes, she wanted to check on him, but not because he was drunk.

She wanted to check on him, *on them*, while she had the chance, for she loathed the way they'd parted.

There was a guard outside, one of the guards who had deposited him on the bed, and he gave Flo a nod and let her in. She walked down a long corridor and when she got to his bedroom she knocked softly and opened the door quietly.

Moonlight lit the room.

Hazin was asleep on top of the bed. In fact, he was just as he had been when she'd left. Flo slipped off his shoes and covered him with a large throw and he stirred.

'I told you,' he said, 'I don't need a nurse.'

'I know you don't,' Flo said. 'And whether or not you

need a friend, tonight I do.' She slipped off her shoes and climbed onto the bed beside him. Without a word, he pulled her in and covered her with the throw.

It wasn't sexy or anything, it was just nice, to lie there in the quiet.

'I'm sorry I didn't tell you I knew who you were.' Flo said.

'It doesn't matter.' He gave her arm a squeeze. 'It was a good night until then.'

'It was.'

'So you were there for Maggie?'

'She wanted to tell Ilyas about the baby.' Flo nodded slowly as she looked back at that night and then sighed. 'I'm going to miss her an awful lot.'

'You'll still see her. She's hardly going to have to save up her frequent flyer miles to come and see you.'

'Perhaps, but it won't be the same. I was so happy when she came back from her year away. I was looking forward to being like an aunty to the baby...'

'You still can be,' he said, and then asked a question. 'Did you used to go out on the town together?'

Flo smiled to herself. 'We met for coffee most days. Maggie's not into clubs.'

'And you are?'

Not any more, Flo thought, but she did not say it.

'So when does your self-imposed exile end?'

Flo lay there and still said nothing.

It had ended with him, but she could not see herself heading back out there.

Something had shifted within her on the very night she had met Hazin, though she hadn't explored it properly and could not do so now, for she doubted that Hazin wanted to hear on this night that she was completely crazy about him.

He misread her silence.

Or not.

For there was sadness in the air; he just didn't put it down to being about him.

'What happened, Flo?' Hazin already knew that her ex had been married but he wanted to hear it from her. 'Why have you been hiding yourself away?'

She hadn't just been hiding, it had been a punishment, one she had inflicted on herself.

'He was married,' Flo said. 'I honestly didn't know, though looking back I should have. I knew he went away on business a lot. At the time, I was fine with it because it was coming up for Christmas...' She thought about it some more. It had actually been a bit of a relief when he'd gone away for he'd liked to see her at short notice and would be put out if she had other plans. On-call sex, really, now she looked back. 'We didn't actually go out that much,' Flo admitted. 'I met him at Dion's and after that it was always bloody hotels.'

'What's wrong with hotels?' Hazin asked.

'Nothing at all, if sex is all you're after. He would sometimes come to my place but it was mainly hotels—he told me his apartment was being renovated. We were always staying in when I wanted to go out.'

'Where?'

'Anywhere, just on a date.'

But the concept of a date was clearly as unfamiliar to him as her aversion to hotels so he asked for more clarification. 'But where would you go?'

'Anywhere. Movies, theatre, meals...'

He yawned and Flo lay there. 'I haven't been on enough dates,' she told him. 'I can see it now.'

Her year off men had served her well.

'How did you find out he was married?' Hazin asked.

She was silent.

'Tell me.'

'I'm too embarrassed to.'

He could feel the tension lock her arms tight against her body. 'Flo,' he said, 'do you know my reputation?'

'I do.'

'Then you must know that not much shocks me.'

Flo had held it in for so long. She remembered the night she and Hazin had met and his kind, non-judgmental smile. She had come close to telling him then and so she told him now.

Hazin was the first person—the only person—she had ever shared this with.

'He came into my department with his wife. She was booked in at a private hospital but it was all happening too fast...' Even with months having gone by, even with the shield of his arms, she could not complete it, but Hazin knew her job and soon worked it out.

'I stand corrected,' he admitted, for he was shocked. 'Bastard.'

They lay there together and he thought about it.

'You didn't have to deliver her?' Hazin checked.

'Oh, God, no, never!' Flo said. 'I hid in the IV cupboard and I never wanted to come out.'

It had been rock bottom for her.

'Then I told my colleague I had a bad period and I needed to go home. I called in sick for two days...'

She looked up and he pulled a face at her ailment choice.

'Well, I guess I could have just pretended to be drunk, as a certain person does when he wants to get out of something.'

They both smiled just a little, but hers wavered when

she recalled that time and the explosion of feelings it had produced.

'It was Christmas Eve and the next day I had to go to my parents' home and pretend to be all happy…'

Hazin frowned. 'I never feign happiness, I'm just a miserable bastard whenever I feel like it.'

'You don't feel like one now.'

He felt lovely, all big and strong and so very kind, and then he said something she did not understand.

'I used to, though.'

'When?'

He thought back to the early months of his marriage, before Petra had taken ill. He had been the dutiful Prince then, attending endless functions with his gorgeous bride. Petra had been very hands on and had liked to get close to the people. At night they would get into this very bed and make love—yet it had not really been love, for he would lie there afterwards in the dark of the night with a hollow longing in his soul for the life he had once led in London.

Yet he could never tell anyone that.

And so he asked Flo a question instead of answering hers. 'Why did you have to pretend to be happy?'

'Because that's what I do,' Flo said.

'Would your parents have been cross with you?'

'No, no, they'd have felt awful for me. It was Christmas,' she said, as if that explained it.

It didn't.

So she tried.

'You do what you can to make it happy for the people you love, especially at Christmas, and me sobbing into the turkey wasn't going to help anyone.'

He lay there, waiting for her to explain further.
It took a moment to realise she had fallen asleep.
Confession really was good for the soul.

CHAPTER SEVEN

IT WAS THE best sleep.

For both of them.

Hazin woke first and he lay there, both liking the feel of her in his arms and dreading the day ahead.

He would be hauled over the coals by his father and asked to explain his behaviour yesterday.

Yet he could not.

His jet had sat at Dubai Airport for hours as he'd toyed with whether or not to attend the wedding.

He had been cross with Maggie for spilling his secrets to Ilyas, yet he understood why she had.

And though a part of him had wanted to be at the wedding, it had been the balcony appearance that Hazin had not been able to face.

The last time he had stood there had been with his young bride, on the day they'd met.

And sitting in Dubai, the thought of the speech on the anniversary of her death had loomed and on a foolish impulse he had decided to do the unthinkable and ensure once and for all that he was removed from the lineage.

Except Ilyas was now in control.

And he wanted Hazin to stand beside him.

Yet Hazin did not know how.

Growing up, he had loathed being the dutiful Prince.

Hazin had felt like a charlatan, for he had known that the poverty in which so many of the people lived was unnecessary. And he had also known of the unrest with the Bedouins under his father's ruthless rule.

Yet the people had loved him.

They always had.

As a young teenager, his father had been giving a speech and the cameras had caught Hazin rolling his eyes.

He had been severely disciplined, but with each lashing, he had—to his father's fury—smiled contentedly.

And, newly married, he and Petra would go into town and dine at the restaurants and actually speak with the locals, who had in turn adored the young couple.

Now his father apologised to the people for his son's sins.

It should be the other way around.

Without words, perhaps, but there was so much good he could do.

Hazin felt Flo stir in his arms.

She would be the best part of this day, Hazin knew.

And he was the best part of hers, for to lie there all warm and rested and to open her eyes to his welcoming smile was such a lovely awakening.

Flo stretched her neck like a swan and reached for his kiss. He met her midway and their lips mingled in an intimate morning caress.

He pulled her up his body and, like Scotch mist rolling in, he slowly engulfed her. Their tongues teased in tender exploration as beneath the rug his hands moved to her breast.

She longed to be naked as they kissed. Flo craved

those fingers stroking her hardened nipple and the palm with which be caressed her bare skin.

And yet it remained at a kiss, for he halted the mingling of their mouths and she could almost taste the regret he left on her lips.

'I have to go,' he told her.

'Do you?' Flo didn't quite believe him.

'I have to go and speak with my father,' Hazin said.

But while his actions yesterday needed to be faced, the truth was that it was all too new and surreal to have someone else in this bed. It took things to a far higher level, though he could not explain that to her, so he applied logic instead. 'And you have your flight to get ready for.'

However gently he did it, Flo knew she was being dismissed.

'What will your father say?' Flo asked as she climbed out of bed.

'Plenty.' Hazin rolled his eyes.

'Did you ever get on?'

'Never,' Hazin said, but then amended, 'For the two weeks while my wedding was being arranged he was more amenable. But that was only because I was dancing to his tune.'

He stood from the bed and gave her a smile—though it was not a smile she liked. It was a smile of farewell. 'Thanks for everything, Flo.'

'I didn't do anything.'

'Well, thanks for looking out for me yesterday when you thought I was drunk.'

'I never did think that, Hazin.'

She had known right away he'd been staging things, and it hadn't all been down to her training. Flo felt a connection with him, though it was clear it was something Hazin didn't want. There was no suggestion that he would see her before she left and no offer to catch up when they were both in London.

'I'll say goodbye, then,' Flo said.

'Goodbye, Flo.'

He might just as well have shaken her hand, Flo thought as she left.

He saw the slight slump of her shoulders and he fought not to call her back as she walked out the door.

It would be the easiest thing to do.

To call her back and blot out the morning and the weeks and months ahead. To fly her back to London on his jet and sex the miles away up in the air.

Yet Hazin knew the easy solution was not the correct one here.

And so he bathed and changed into a robe and put on his *keffiyeh*, and when Mahmoud, the King's vizier, called and said that King Ahmed wished to speak to him, Hazin was ready.

It was not a welcoming committee that waited.

His father sat at his huge desk, with Mahmoud standing beside him. The surprise was that his mother was standing there too.

'Mumia!' Hazin greeted her with the Arabic word for 'Mummy', but it dripped sarcasm for he had not used that word even as a child.

He hadn't been taught to and he'd certainly never had the chance to.

Being back made his skin crawl, for he could remember long nights in the nursery, crying out, only to be ignored or met by a stern nanny.

'Discipline him,' his mother would hiss on her rare visits, and well he remembered her tone now.

She stared coolly at the son she had reluctantly borne

and then addressed him. 'Your behaviour yesterday was despicable. Many esteemed guests witnessed your display.'

'You're not upset that I might have upset your son and his new wife?' Hazin checked. 'Just that I embarrassed you in front of guests.'

'You always embarrass me, Hazin. You do nothing right.'

'For such a rebel, I excelled at school.'

'You hardly needed qualifications to support yourself,' the Queen sniffed. 'Perhaps you might wish you had gone to university now, when you hear what the King has to say.'

Hazin looked at his father as the King spoke. 'My strong recommendation is that you will be disinherited. I want the people to see the consequences of your despicable behaviour. However...' King Ahmed's face twisted as the new order in the Palace choked him. 'Ilyas is determined that your title will remain. Your brother has more faith in you than I do. Though that is hardly a compliment for I have none. I would wash my hands of you with satisfaction.'

'You washed your hands of me before I was even born,' Hazin responded, then looked at the Queen—she did not deserve the title of Mother. 'And you washed your hands of me on the day that I was,' he finished, looking at the King.

He had been fed by wet nurses and visited by his mother on rare occasions. And when at six years of age he had kicked up, he'd been offed to a country where he didn't even know the language.

Hazin was angry now.

Furious, in fact, not just about his childhood but for the utter lack of support shown to his late wife. Once she had become ill they had treated Petra as if she had been a poor choice of bride—even though they had been the ones who had chosen her.

Yes, his hate ran deep and it built the more she spoke.

'It does not have to be Ilyas's choice,' the Queen pointed out. 'You can always step down.'

They wanted him to, Hazin realised. They wanted him gone before Ilyas returned from the desert.

It was their only chance at wresting back control, for there was safety in numbers. He thought of Ilyas standing alone against these two.

He had no doubt now in Ilyas, and he was a formidable force indeed. But these two were pure poison, and not afraid to use it.

His brother had said he wanted him there by his side.

But Hazin didn't know Ilyas.

Simply, he did not know him.

Yet there was intrinsic trust between them. He thought back to the coffee bar and that stir of relief when Ilyas had told him that things would change.

So he spoke in a steady voice to the Queen, for his decision was made. 'I shall not be stepping down,' Hazin said, and he watched her blink rapidly. 'And, given that you no longer have the power to disinherit me, there's really no point to this conversation.'

'Oh, but there is,' Ahmed said, and he played his final card. 'If you refuse to step down, Hazin, then it is time to step up. The formal invitations for the anniversary of Petra's death are about to be sent. The date is the twenty third of December and the ceremony shall commence at two p.m.'

And Hazin stood there as his father outlined Hazin's own personal hell.

'We thought it fitting that Petra's family be there as

you open the new oncology wing. They shall be on the stage beside you. Naturally, it shall be televised, for it has been a long time since our people have heard from their missing, errant Prince. I am sure they will listen closely to what you have to say for yourself.' The King watched the sweat bead on his son's brow and with a black smile he looked over at his vizier. 'Not to worry, though, Mahmoud is working on your speech.'

Hazin turned and walked away.

Through the guarded doors and into the grand entrance, where there hung the portrait of him and Petra, taunting him. How the hell could he face her parents after all he had done in the years since he had last seen them? How could he sit on a stage, with the world watching, and deliver a speech about how much he'd loved and missed his wife. He looked into her chocolate eyes and did not know how to face the day. He just did not know, but as he stared at Petra he remembered her kindness.

Such kindness, and it had been so alien to Hazin that he had not known how to accept it at first.

And, no, his heart had not raced in her presence or at the thought of her, but he had done all he could to return the gentleness of her nature.

I want to do the right thing by you but I don't know how.

He said it in his head, but Petra only smiled back for her smile was fixed on the wall.

The easiest thing to do would be to head back to bed and bury himself in Flo, but that would not honour either of these women. He turned to leave.

It was a familiar sight at the Palace—Hazin flying out the day after he had flown in.

But it was not familiar to Flo.

She was on the balcony, drinking in the view and watching the constant activity as various dignitaries left, when she saw him stride across the bridge and board his jet without a backward glance.

No goodbye, no kiss.

Nothing.

She watched the plane with its black and silver tail hurtle down the runway and lift into the clear blue sky.

And she watched until the speck in the distance had gone, scanning the sky in the ridiculous hope that the plane might return. He might realise that he had left something important behind—her heart. He might change his mind and come back to the Palace…

Of course not.

And so to life without him.

CHAPTER EIGHT

DECEMBER.

It had always been Flo's favourite month.

Not any more.

She had worked a lot of late shifts in the first two weeks, but more so that she would have a genuine excuse not to attend the many functions and get-togethers that came with this time of year.

The unbelievable had happened and Christmas had lost its gloss.

She had finished up work yesterday to commence her long-awaited leave and was determined to inject some enthusiasm into the season. Yet she decorated the tree and her tiny flat with something more akin to grim determination than enthusiasm.

Then Flo headed out to make a start on her Christmas shopping.

The bus stopped right beside the chocolate café. If Maggie had still been working there, Flo would have dropped in for a hot chocolate and a gossip.

Then, after her shopping, she might well have ended up back there again.

They spoke online often enough, but it was in the day-to-day things that Flo missed her an awful lot.

The shops were all decked out for Christmas yet Flo's

shopping wasn't done. She traipsed around the various stores, but the music was too loud and the crowds overwhelming. As well as that, she had seen what was surely the perfect necklace for Maggie.

Yet, just as she had been admiring it, Flo had thought of the stunning jewels that Maggie now had access to and had put it back.

Somehow she could not get in the mood.

Last Christmas had been awful.

This one was faring no better.

Well, that wasn't strictly true.

Last year at this time she had been happy, decorating her tiny flat and dashing to the shops to get the perfect presents for family and friends and her now ex-boyfriend.

Yes, this time last year she had been busy and happy.

It was Christmas Eve that had been hell.

She had felt so ashamed yet, looking back, she hadn't cried tears over the loss of him.

Yet, after one night with Hazin, Flo had cried.

And she had cried over him several times since.

Today, as she took the bus back to her flat, it felt as if it could be one of those times.

The bus made its way along the busy London street and Flo looked down and saw Dion's.

She hadn't been back since that night when he had first turned her life around.

According to the gossip columns, neither had Hazin.

That morning, after the wedding, when she had woken in his bed and they had shared that lovely kiss, had been the last time she had seen or heard from him.

Flo had found out from Maggie that he hadn't been back to Zayrinia either.

It would seem he really did not want to deliver that speech or stand with is brother.

He was off in the Caribbean, according to the last gossip rag Flo had read.

Flo let herself into her flat. She pulled off her boots and scarf and refused to cry over a man who clearly had no real interest in her.

Another one.

Only with Hazin it didn't feel the same as it had with other boyfriends, for when she had been with him, his interest in her had felt real.

Get real! Flo told herself.

It had been three months.

She pulled out her laptop, trying not to think about Hazin, and to decide what to get Maggie for Christmas. Flo had left it rather too late to post something, so she'd have to spend a small fortune for a necklace Maggie might not even want.

Suddenly Maggie messaged her. Great minds think alike, Flo thought.

Free to chat?

A few seconds later there was Maggie, smiling from the screen. Her red hair was thick and glossy and she was clearly rocking those pregnancy hormones.

'You look amazing,' Flo said. 'Three weeks to go!'

'It feels like for ever,' Maggie sighed.

'How's it all going?'

'Very well,' Maggie said. 'Well, at least I think so…'

'What's wrong?'

'Nothing. I just…' Maggie closed her eyes. 'Flo, do you remember when you asked if you could deliver me?'

'Yes, and you said that you could think of nothing worse than that.'

'I could think of nothing better now,' Maggie told her.

'Are you okay?'

'Honestly, yes. I'm getting the best care and I really am fine. I'm getting all worked up, though. I have to deliver at the Palace, unless something goes wrong, of course. But as well as the Palace doctor there has to be a Palace elder present at the birth.'

Flo held in her own thoughts about that.

Maggie didn't need them.

At the end of the day, she was giving birth to the future King. Of course there would be certain customs that had to be adhered to.

Yet Maggie was a very private person.

Late pregnancy was often a difficult time, especially given that Maggie was in a new country and didn't speak the language, and it made sense that she would want someone from home with her.

But Flo wasn't sure if she wanted to go.

Not that she said it out loud; instead she pointed out a fact. 'Maggie, what happens if the baby's late? First babies often are and I'm due back at work on the fifth of January.'

'I know. It would just be so nice to have you here for a while.'

Flo thought about it.

She wanted to be there for her friend but she loved Christmas, and the thought of not spending it with her family was daunting.

'Flo, it honestly would be a holiday,' Maggie said. 'We can go out and you can go off exploring. I'll take you out to the desert where Ilyas and I met.'

'You're thirty-seven weeks pregnant.'

'And there are helicopters lined up outside like a taxi rank. Though I do have a couple of functions to attend, so long as the baby's not here. I just…' Maggie hesitated. 'I'm asking too much. I know how much you love Christmas and being with your family.'

Flo had always loved Christmas—the tree, the scents, the gorgeous dinner—but she had been feeling so low of late.

Flo needed to think about it, yet she could see the pleading in Maggie's eyes and she was absolutely useless at saying no, or even asking for some time.

'Of course you're not asking too much,' Flo said. 'I'd love to come.'

Maggie gave a squeal of delight. 'When?'

'How soon do you want me?'

'Now!' Maggie said, and started to speak of arrangements. 'Don't bring a thing. I've got a wardrobe of robes and I'll get Kumu to—' but Flo cut in.

'You'll have to message me the details. If I'm going to be flying to Zayrinia at short notice then I need to hit the shops now.'

'I just said you don't have to bring anything.'

'I've got my family's presents to get,' Flo pointed out.

This was more like it, Flo thought as she entered the huge store that she'd so listlessly walked around just a couple of hours before.

On the bus ride over, she had thought about it and a working holiday in Zayrinia, and delivering a future King, wouldn't look too bad on her résumé.

Hazin might be there; after all, he had that dreaded speech to give.

He wasn't the sole reason for her cheery mood. She

and Maggie were very close, but the chance to see Hazin again was certainly a factor.

She simply couldn't get him out of her mind, though she had to now because Flo had so much to do.

So much!

Yet this time around it all happened with ease.

Her brothers, sisters, parents, nieces and nephews were soon off her list and Flo left the bags at a counter to collect later.

Ilyas?

Impossible.

So he got a box of dark-chocolate-covered ginger.

A big one, though.

Maggie had become newly impossible to buy for, but she utterly refused to think like that, so Flo went back to the necklace and bought it, along with a book that she knew Maggie would enjoy.

And then Flo went to the place she longed to be most—the baby floor.

Despite seeing, holding and smelling newborns each and every day, it was never too much for Flo.

Shopping for her friend's baby was an utter delight, though she would love to be shopping for her own.

Flo had wanted a baby as far back as she could remember.

Every doll she had begged for at Christmas and birthdays had proven a secret disappointment when she'd finally held them, for she had longed for them to be real.

It wasn't like she was peering into prams and longing to scoop the babies out, it was just that she hoped to be a mother one day.

Flo knew Maggie was having a little boy but, rather than blue, she loved the more neutral mint greens and pale lemons and she searched for just that.

And then she found it—a little playsuit in the palest green with the face of a rabbit, or dog, or something of that nature on the front.

It wasn't very regal, but it was gorgeous.

And he got a teddy, because from the little she knew of the al-Razim brothers, they hadn't exactly been plied with toys as children and a palace could be a cold and lonely place.

So she splurged and got him a little play mat and a rattle too in the shape of a ladybird.

Done.

Not quite.

Hazin!

Her mother had trained her well, and of course there must be spare presents for the unexpected and, in this case, much-hoped-for, guest.

For that was what he was, Flo thought, more a guest in the Palace than a much-loved son.

Hazin had been born a spare.

So an extra box of chocolate ginger would not cut it, Flo thought, even as she bought some for him anyway.

She stood in the middle of the store as that Hazin-shaped wave hit her again.

It had swamped her on too many occasions of late.

What were you supposed to get for someone you desperately fancied but who might not even be there. What present were you supposed to get a man who could afford absolutely anything?

Flo couldn't fight it any more.

While it might have been sex in a hotel to him, it had been far more than that to her.

She was crazy about him.

That night in his arms in the Palace where nothing had happened had been the most amazing of her life.

She loved sex, but Flo had found out that night just how nice it was to hold someone and be held for no other reason than to hold and be held.

It had never happened to her before.

She'd been held before, of course, but there had never been one without the other.

Until Hazin.

She *had* to get a present for him, just in case he was there, but what?

It had to be light, Flo thought.

But she wanted more of Hazin, not less…

And suddenly Flo knew what to buy.

It could prove an expensive mistake, Flo thought as she grabbed her many bags and headed off to make her purchase.

And it could prove a rather lonely exercise.

But then at least she'd know.

CHAPTER NINE

ZAYRINIA WAS BEAUTIFUL, Flo thought as the plane came in to land and she got a glimpse of the Palace sitting atop the canyon on the very edge of the desert. She could absolutely see why Maggie had been drawn to the place.

Flo was nervous, though.

Last time she had flown here it had been on a private jet and they had landed in the grounds of the Palace. She had been with Maggie, revelling in the bliss of Il-yas's jet and so excited about the wedding. This time, an itinerary had been sent to her by Kumu. She was being flown first class, which was terribly exciting, although a part of Flo would have preferred to be back in economy and the flight paid for by herself.

Just a friend visiting a friend.

Flo's itinerary stated she would be met at Zayrinia airport and then be taken straight to the Palace.

It was as impersonal as that.

But as she stepped into a small lounge area, the first person she saw was Maggie.

Hugely pregnant and waving to her friend.

Although it was the VIP lounge rather than the chocolate café of old, immediately they clicked back into familiar ways.

'I didn't think you were coming to meet me,' Flo admitted.

'Didn't Kumu tell you that you would be met? She told me she'd sent you all the details.'

'The itinerary just said I'd be taken to the palace,' Flo said. 'It didn't mention you.'

'Well, Kumu's super-organised and was no doubt making provisions in case I was in labour. Otherwise, of course I'd be here.'

The Palace was as beautiful as when Flo had left it and she was shown to her former, now-familiar suite.

'I told you not to worry about clothes,' Maggie said when she saw Flo's cases waiting in her suite. 'It's all robes here and I have loads.'

They had always borrowed and swapped clothes. As Maggie had pointed out, it was a bit pointless to fork out for a new wardrobe when she had so many.

'I just didn't know what to pack.'

That wasn't true.

Flo had packed plenty and had warned the maids that she wanted to unpack the cases herself, because they didn't contain many clothes—her luggage was mostly filled with presents.

They went for a walk in the gardens and though cool it was nice to breathe in fresh air and to walk for a while after being on a plane.

'I can't believe you're here,' Maggie said.

'Nor can I.' Flo smiled.

It had all been a huge rush to get here—dropping Christmas presents off to her family as she'd told them of her sudden change of plans.

Her mother, Flo could tell, while excited for her, had been disappointed that she wouldn't be there for

Christmas, but they had promised they would have a big dinner as soon as Flo got back.

'How's work?' Maggie asked.

'It's great but always too busy,' Flo said. 'I seem to spend more time writing up notes than anything.'

'Well, you don't have to write any notes up on me. I'm just so glad there's a chance you'll be here when he's born.'

'I'll be here whenever he arrives,' Flo said.

She had made up her mind.

Just as she wouldn't leave a woman in the second stage of labour, neither would she walk away from her friend so close to the end. 'I told the unit manager that I'm staying until the baby's here. I'm not officially due back until the fifth but we can work something out if your little man isn't here by then.'

'Oh, I hope he is,' Maggie sighed, and finally explained some of what was on her mind. 'I told you that an elder has to be present at the birth?'

Flo nodded.

Since Maggie had asked her to be there, Flo had looked into things and had thought through her approach. Instead of fighting the system and getting Maggie all worked up in the process, she was practical instead.

'Maggie, you are giving birth to the future King. If there wasn't someone official present, I could well be smuggling him in under my robe.'

Maggie smiled but Flo could tell she was still concerned.

'I'll talk to the Palace doctor and find out what *has* to happen and how we can all work around it.'

'Will you?'

'Of course I will,' Flo said. 'You're going to have a fantastic birth, I just know it.'

'Thanks.' Maggie's smile was more relaxed now. 'And we're going to have an amazing time. Ilyas has to go to the desert next week and, as long as the baby is behaving, we can spend the day at the tent!'

'Where you two met,' Flo said.

'Well, not met exactly,' Maggie said. 'Where he had me brought to him!'

They both laughed at all that had happened.

'So what's been happening with you?'

'Oh, you know,' Flo said. 'More of the same.'

'Meaning?'

'I've just been really busy with work.'

'You're always busy with work,' Maggie said. 'But you still manage to squeeze in fun. Are you seeing anyone?'

'Not really.'

Flo knew she was being evasive, yet she was also telling the truth. It had been almost a year since she'd gone out with anyone. Hazin had been her only slip-up.

And they had never really gone out.

It had been just a one-night stand really, except to Flo it felt so much more than that.

But instead of talking about her lack of a love life, Flo asked about Christmas plans.

'There aren't any,' Maggie said. 'It's just another day here. Ilyas and I have to go to Idihr a few days before…'

'That's fine,' Flo said. 'I don't need a babysitter.'

'And then there's Hazin's speech on the twenty-third.' Flo felt her stomach clench as Maggie mentioned his name. 'If he gets here.'

She looked at Maggie as they walked.

They chatted about a lot.

A lot.

Yet Flo simply did not know how to chat about this.

'*If* he gets here?' Flo checked.

'It would seem that he's still doing his best to get dis-inherited. He was in the Caribbean the last Ilyas heard. No doubt partying hard.'

Maggie knew no more than her, Flo realised.

No one really knew Hazin.

Not his parents.

Or his brother.

And clearly not the King's vizier, Mahmoud, who, a few days later emailed the first draft of Hazin's speech, to be delivered on the tenth anniversary of Petra's death.

Hazin lay on top of a bed, drinking iced sparkling water, but it did not cool his building temper as he read through the words.

The proposed speech belittled the brief joy Petra had brought to the people of Zayrinia and it cited her death as the cause for Hazin's reckless years.

It made *her* into an excuse for *him*.

Hazin flung the glass of water across the room and it smashed against the wall. But it brought Hazin no relief.

He then walked out onto the beach. The water was azure and crystal clear and the beach so white, unlike at home, where the sands were a rusty, beautiful orange.

Home.

It had never really felt like Zayrinia was home, but there was no denying that it called to him now, for the commemoration of Petra's life was just a few days away.

And he had decided to attend.

Hazin intended to fly in on the morning of the ceremony and back out that same night, though he had not told Ilyas that, for he knew he would try to coax him into staying longer.

There was little chance of that.

As for the speech, Hazin would not be reading from Mahmoud's draft. He wanted to honour Petra, but to stand there and say such empty words would dishonour her memory.

Hazin called his brother.

'I write my own speeches, Ilyas.'

'Since when?' Ilyas clipped. 'You're never here to make one.'

Hazin had no smart reply to that.

'You had better be here,' Ilyas warned. 'And sober this time, unlike at my wedding.'

His brother had no idea that Hazin didn't drink.

But Flo did.

After one night together she had worked it out. But he could not think of that now and so instead he tore the current version of his speech apart. 'What is this about the black sheep, and grief making a foolish guide?'

'Hazin,' Ilyas sighed. 'We've thought long and hard and decided that your reckless ways cannot be ignored.'

'So you make Petra's death into an excuse for me? How dare you use her in that way?'

'No one is using Petra but, for whatever reason, since Petra died you *have* gone off the rails.'

'Rubbish.'

'Hazin, your brother is the person who is honest with you, not the one who believes you.'

He did not need some old saying stuffed down his throat and Hazin told his brother that. 'You have the gall to criticise me when you had your harem?' Hazin pointed out. 'All you had to do was pull a bell—at least I indulge in a bit flirting and conversation.'

'Don't try and condone your behaviour,' Ilyas said. 'From all I have read there is little conversation and no flirting where your lovers are concerned.'

Hazin closed his eyes for there had been plenty to read and most of the kiss-and-tell stories were true. He was on the cover of trashy magazines, and there were articles and photos all over the Internet.

Not recently, though, and Ilyas admitted that at least. 'But there have been no scandals of late.'

'No.'

'Can you keep it that way until the ceremony at least?'

'I don't need you to tell me how to act,' Hazin said as he looked out at the lonely island where he had holed himself away from the world.

An idyllic romantic retreat—without the romance.

What Ilyas had said was true, there had been no scandals recently. But that was not because he was attempting to redeem his name, neither was it because all temptations had been removed.

They simply no longer held any appeal for him.

'I need to go.' Ilyas cut into his thoughts. 'Not only am I sick of discussing your sex life, Hazin, but I am taking Maggie and her friend out to the desert abode today.'

'Playing tourist guide,' Hazin sneered.

'Not playing,' Ilyas responded. 'I am meeting with the Bedouin leaders to solidify our political ties and to invite them to join a roundtable so they can play a bigger role in shaping the country's future.'

Hazin frowned, because this had been something

the Bedouins had long been pushing for yet his father had always dismissed the notion.

But Ilyas had more to say.

'I also happen to enjoy my wife's company and I am more than pleased to show Flo where we first met.'

'Flo?'

'Maggie's friend. You would have met her at the wedding...' Ilyas paused. 'Oh, that's right, you were too drunk to attend.' Ilyas stopped the lectures then. 'Flo's also a midwife and has been staying with us. I think Maggie is nervous about giving birth with an elder present and—'

'Ilyas,' Hazin interrupted. 'Just as you don't want to discuss my sex life, neither do I need to hear about Maggie's plans for her labour.'

'Fine.'

Hazin was curt, but there was no emotional bond between them and not a single memory Hazin could call on that softened his brother. He had always been forbidding and distant. Certainly it was too late to be friends and have cosy chats but, more importantly, Hazin did not want to hear about Flo.

Not now.

'Enjoy your time in the desert,' Hazin said, and rang off.

He stripped and placed his phone on his clothes, then headed into the surf and swam for the best part of an hour. But no matter how far or how hard he swam, he could not outswim his own thoughts.

Flo was in Zayrinia.

How was he supposed to feel at hearing that news?

There would be warmth and laughter for once at the Palace, and if he did not care about her so much she might even have served as a pleasant distraction.

Yet he did care.

Hazin wanted to address how he felt about Flo, *after* the anniversary.

Not before.

First up, he *had* to finally do the right thing by Petra.

CHAPTER TEN

ILYAS CERTAINLY WASN'T playing tour guide.

When they arrived at the desert abode he disappeared to prepare for his meeting and Maggie showed Flo around while the maids set up for lunch. 'This is where I slept on the first night I was here.'

'And by the second you were in Ilyas's bed,' Flo reminded her.

It was gorgeous, with a huge satin-draped bed and a luxurious bathing area. It was mysterious and beautiful and Flo could absolutely now see why Maggie loved to come here. 'When you've told me that you and Ilyas were heading off to the desert, I've always felt a bit sorry for you, but I won't now.'

They stepped back into the main living area and Flo was entranced. 'I don't think I've ever seen anywhere more beautiful.' And that was saying something, having come from the Palace. But it was just so lavishly furnished. A huge fire was in the centre of the tent and the flue ran up to the ceiling. On the walls hung tapestries and the rugs on the floor were so plump and inviting that you could easily sleep on them. Ilyas joined them and they sat on cushions around a low table and ate from an array of tajines.

The food was smoky and delicious. Flo's favourite was a mild chicken and date curry, which she tucked into as Ilyas told her why he would be leaving them for the rest of the day.

'I am to speak with the Bedouins and invite their representatives to join us at some Palace meetings.'

'Do you think they'll come?' Flo asked, surprised that Ilyas had even said this much. He was very formal, or at least he had been when they had met at the wedding, but recently he had opened up a little.

Perhaps he had realised just what good friends she and Maggie were, Flo thought as he answered her question.

'I expect so. Being consulted and given a voice is something they have wanted for a long time,' Ilyas said. 'I have forged a good relationship with them over the years but there is a lot of history. It is not only the Bedouins whose trust I hope to win, though. That is why Maggie and I are heading to Idihr tomorrow. There has been a lot of damage done to our standing with neighbouring countries. I hope Hazin changes his mind about returning on a more permanent basis; there is a lot of work that needs to be done.'

At the mention of his name, Flo had to fight to keep her features impassive as she asked, 'Do you think he will?'

'I doubt it,' Ilyas admitted. 'I spoke to him this morning and I can't even pin him down to an arrival time for the memorial event for his late wife.'

'He'll be here for that,' Maggie said assuredly.

'I am not so sure.' Ilyas shook his head. 'He has few fond memories of Zayrinia and little desire to come back. Whenever he does return...' he gave a slight smile in Flo's direction '… I am sure my wife will have told you he tends to take out the yacht.'

It was a little tease about how he and Maggie had first met.

'Ah, yes,' Flo said. 'Well, perhaps the yacht will need to go in for a long service after three months in the Caribbean.'

There was, though she fought it, a slight edge to her voice and she watched as Ilyas's perceptive eyes narrowed a touch.

'Is it really three months?' he asked. 'I admit, I haven't been counting.'

'Well, Maggie was six months pregnant at the wedding and she's due any day now. I have a midwife's mind rather than a mathematical one.'

She'd got out of that one.

Just!

But it was becoming harder and harder not to reveal just how much she liked Hazin.

'Your desert abode is beautiful,' Flo said, quickly changing the subject.

'You should see it at night.' Maggie gave a wistful sigh. 'When it's dark and the fire is burning and all the lanterns are lit and the music…' She stopped and looked at Ilyas. 'Why don't we stay tonight?'

'I can't.' Ilyas shook his head. 'I have to be at the Palace for an engagement tonight and I am in back-to-back meetings all day tomorrow. Still, there's no reason you two can't stay.' He must have seen Flo's flicker of concern at the thought of being deep in the desert with a heavily pregnant woman for he immediately addressed it. 'Once I get to the Palace I will send the helicopter straight back. If there is a need to return sooner you would only be an hour away.'

A taxi ride to the hospital really, by the time they turned up! 'Sounds wonderful.'

And it truly was.

The afternoon was spent in the kitchen.
With much laughter, Flo learnt from one of the maids how to prepare the date and chicken curry and then she and Maggie went for a gentle walk around the tent.

It was a feast for the eyes outside too.

There were beautiful Arabian horses and even a little white foal. His tail was high and his long legs so slender that he looked as if he should be on a carrousel.

'Oh, I want him,' Flo breathed.

'Be careful speaking like that in front of Ilyas,' Maggie teased. 'Or that cute little creature might be a surprise gift waiting on your doorstep when you return home.'

It was such a glorious afternoon. Ilyas returned from his meeting with the Bedouin elders and then headed back to the Palace, and soon it was just the two of them.

There was a deep sense of peace here that Flo had never known. It was such bliss to lie on the cushions and chat with her friend as the fire bathed them in a warm glow and they spoke about life in Zayrinia.

'Do you miss home at all?' Flo asked.

'I miss you and my friends but…' Maggie thought for a moment. 'I haven't really had a home as such since I was seven.'

Flo nodded.

She understood completely what Maggie was saying. Maggie didn't have any family, whereas Flo was very close to hers.

'It's going to be so odd, not seeing them at Christmas,' Flo admitted.

'I don't miss Christmas either,' Maggie sighed. 'It's the time of year I always miss my mum the most. It's kind of nice to bypass it.'

'You can't bypass it, though, Maggie,' Flo said. 'You're always going to miss her.'

'I know I am. I guess Christmas just isn't the big deal to me that it is to you. I could have the staff try and make a dinner for us...'

Flo laughed. 'Please don't. I'm very specific with my trimmings. Mum's freezing me a huge dinner and I'm going to have it when I get back.' She smiled at the thought and then frowned. 'Have there been any deliveries for me?'

'No.' Maggie shook her head. 'Are you expecting one?'

'Not really.' Flo shrugged. 'Mum said that we'd do presents and things when I get back, I just thought she might have sent something for me to open on the day.'

Flo resisted an unhappy sigh and reminded herself that she was twenty-nine! But it was still quite a daunting prospect to have nothing to open for Christmas. Clearly Maggie had given it little thought but she had hoped her mum would have sent something. Still, there was one thing that would certainly cheer Christmas up.

'You might have a Christmas baby!' Flo said.

'Perhaps, but I really want to have the baby tomorrow,'

'Why?'

'Because I'd like to have you here for some time after he comes,' Maggie said, and then she gave a cheeky smile as she admitted another truth. 'And I want to get out of the trip to Idihr as well as the hospital opening.'

'I can write you a note from your midwife to say you

can't possibly attend,' Flo joked, but then, more seriously, she asked a question. 'Why don't you want to go?'

'Well, Idihr will be lovely but it's going to be a very long day. Then it's the hospital opening the next day and it will take for ever. Still, it's so important to the people...' Maggie admitted to a further truth. 'I'm terrified my waters will break.'

'Well, labour usually starts with contractions and they don't generally break with a sudden gush...'

'It *could* happen, though.' Maggie sighed. 'I'm going to sit at the back for the hospital opening and the trip to Idihr is an informal one. Ilyas says that Queen Atisha has had five children...'

'You'll be fine,' Flo said. 'But if it's really working you up, perhaps it might be time to stay home.'

'I'll think about it,' Maggie agreed.

'Do you really think Hazin will come for the opening?' Flo asked, because Maggie had sounded so sure that he would when she'd spoken about it with Ilyas.

'I don't know,' Maggie now admitted. 'No one knows. Ilyas has tried to talk to him but never gets anywhere. Hazin doesn't get close to anyone.'

'He spoke to you on the yacht that day,' Flo pointed out.

'Ah, but only when he thought he'd never have to see me again.'

'How is he with you now?'

'Flo, I haven't seen him since the wedding, and that was just for a moment when he arrived half-drunk. Hazin will do what Hazin does.' Maggie looked at her. 'Please don't like him.'

'But I do.'

'Then please don't act on it, Flo—he's a rake. Well,

he's been lovely to me and everything but that was only because he didn't fancy me.'

'Maybe I should tell Ilyas I like him so Hazin can be waiting with a bow on my doorstep when I get home,' Flo said, making light of her feelings.

It was odd.

Flo had squeezed out all the details from Maggie when she had come back pregnant from her round-the-world trip.

Maggie, certain that she and Ilyas were over and scared to be having a Royal's baby, had told Flo everything.

Yet Flo could not tell her this.

It wasn't because she was ashamed of it, as had been her reason for not telling a soul about the married man.

It was more that she felt she had to protect whatever fragile flame she and Hazin had.

And exposing them could not help, Flo knew. Even if she ached to confide in her friend. Even if she yearned to eke out whatever information she could about him, Flo felt it better to keep what had happened between her and Hazin private for now.

It was a gorgeous night and a really wonderful retreat, just what they had both needed, but all too soon the chopper was landing them back at the Palace.

It really was stunning and so vast.

A plane was landing and there was another waiting to take off.

'The Flying Royals,' Maggie called them as they disembarked, and then she held her stomach.

'I'm having one.'

Flo felt her stomach and all Maggie was having was wishful thinking along with a mild Braxton Hicks contraction, and she gave a slight cackle. 'No, Maggie, you're not.'

There was no sign of the baby making a move anytime soon.

'I'm going to have to go to Idihr, aren't I?' Maggie sighed as they walked across a pretty bridge from the helipad that would take them back to the palace.

Yes, Maggie was Royal now.

'Maybe not. It's your antenatal check tomorrow. If things are starting to move along you'll have a good reason not to go.'

As they walked into the Palace, Ilyas came down the main staircase to the grand entrance to welcome back his wife, which he did with a kiss, and then Maggie asked what he was doing there. 'I thought you had meetings all day.'

'I do.' Ilyas nodded. 'But Hazin's plane just came in. I want to see how he is and if there are any last-minute things he wants added in for the opening.'

Flo didn't know what to do. A part of her wanted to go and hide in her room and have him find out she was here when she wasn't around to see his reaction.

Another part, though, wanted to see his face when he found out.

In the end there was no reaction at all.

He walked in scowling, when the Hazin she knew was always pleasant.

Hazin felt he had actually walked into hell, for Flo, Maggie and Ilyas were standing beneath a huge portrait of himself and his late wife. Everything he was trying to separate was there together in his line of vision.

'Hi,' he said to the gathered trio. His tone was dry

as he kept on walking. 'I really don't need a welcoming committee.'

'You don't have one,' Ilyas said. 'Flo and Maggie have just got back from their trip. I came out to meet them.'

That wasn't true, Flo thought. Ilyas had just told Maggie he had come out to greet his brother.

There was no warmth between the brothers, she thought.

None.

But at least Ilyas tried. 'Would you like to join us for dinner, Hazin?' he offered.

Flo found that she was holding her breath.

'No,' Hazin said. 'Thanks.'

The simple words came in two separate sentences. Even an attempt at politeness had to be forced.

'Please join us, Hazin,' Maggie pushed. 'It would be nice for us all…' She didn't get to finish as Hazin gave a terse shake of his head.

'I already have plans for tonight.'

Hazin did indeed have plans.

As he stalked off to his apartment, Hazin nodded his thanks to the maids who were sorting out his luggage but then asked if they could please leave.

He waited until the doors closed on them and then let out a tense breath.

That had been hell.

This was hell.

He walked through to the bedroom to get to the balcony but, of course, he had to pass the bed.

Flo was the only other woman to have slept with him there—not that she could have known that.

Guilt clawed at his throat like fingers and he loosened his tie.

Hazin hadn't been lying about having plans for tonight when he had declined Ilyas's offer to join them for dinner.

He was dining with Petra's parents.

Hazin did not want to have to meet them for the first time in many years on a stage in front of a gathered crowd.

Instead, he had called them and Petra's father had invited him to come to dinner.

It was going to be a long and difficult night.

CHAPTER ELEVEN

It was certainly a long and difficult night for Flo.

Knowing that Hazin was here in the Palace had her on high alert and caught in the vague hope that he might make contact.

Yet why would he?

Hazin had left Zayrinia last time without so much as a goodbye, and on his return had barely graced her with a glance.

Flo had fallen asleep, trying to work him out, and had awoken none the wiser.

Breakfast was delivered by a smiling maid. Flo sat up and a bed tray consisting of fragrant tea, tiny pastries and a lovely fruit platter was placed over her lap.

Flo could only pick at it.

This morning it was Maggie's antenatal check. Her due date was days away, though first babies were often late.

Maggie, who had first thought it would be awkward having a friend as a midwife, was now a lot more relaxed about it. Flo had spoken with the Palace doctor and also the elder who had to be present for the birth. They were both charming. The doctor did indeed have to, if at all possible, deliver the future King. If there were complications and a Caesarean was required, he would be present in the hospital theatre. 'However...' he had smiled at Flo '...if things are going well, you don't have to rush to call me.'

He really had been kind and understanding and he wanted the same for Maggie as Flo did—a wonderful, uncomplicated birth.

Flo had given in on the few clothes she had brought and was now more at ease about borrowing Maggie's robes. They were so comfortable and light and today she selected one in a deep jade green and tied her hair up high.

There was a flutter of nerves in her stomach as she made her way through the Palace, in case she saw Hazin. Flo had decided that if she did then it was time for her pride to kick in and to coldly ignore him.

Of course, now she had decided that, Hazin was nowhere to be seen. She smiled at the guard and knocked on the door to the suite where Maggie lived and was let in by one of the maids, who explained in broken English that Maggie was bathing.

'That's fine.'

Flo took a seat in the lounge and looked around the exquisite furnishings but all she could see was the complete lack of Christmas.

She wasn't homesick as such for she had spoken with her family regularly while she'd been away and she was loving being here....

Flo was just homesick for Christmas.

As glum as she had been back in London, with Christmas just a few days away, excitement would surely by now have been kicking in as she rushed to the shops to get last-minute things for her mum.

'Hi, there.' Maggie came in wearing a bathing robe with her hair wrapped in a towel. 'I have to get my hair and make-up done later so there didn't seem much point in getting dressed.'

'None at all!' Flo beamed.

'I have to say,' Maggie admitted as they headed through to the bedroom, 'it is so less awkward seeing you for my antenatal checks than I thought it would be.'

'Good,' Flo said, 'but I have to say, the Palace doctor is very nice. He delivered Ilyas and Hazin.'

'Really?'

'And I can see now why you need an elder present,' Flo said cheekily as she checked the specimen Maggie had provided and was relieved to see it was all clear. 'It's hard to believe their parents ever had sex!'

Maggie laughed as Flo spoke on.

'Are they not the coldest people you have ever met?' Flo said as she took out her blood-pressure machine. 'I saw her the other day and she stared right through me.'

At least Hazin had scowled when he'd seen her, Flo thought. The Queen had ignored her so completely that Flo had felt like a ghost, utterly invisible to those noble eyes.

'She's actually better than she was,' Maggie said as she sat on the bed while Flo checked her blood pressure. 'She speaks to me occasionally now and King Ahmed seems to be accepting the transition a little better. He's not in the best of health,' Maggie added.

'They might even be relieved to hand over the reins a bit.'

'Not that they would ever admit it,' Maggie said as Flo took off the cuff.

'Your blood pressure is perfect. You do look tired, though.'

'I didn't sleep much last night.'

'You have a perfect excuse not to go today. No one

would blame you a bit for staying home and putting your feet up rather than being out on official business.'

'I know.' Maggie nodded. 'But I doubt I'll want to leave the baby for a while after he's born. Ilyas is trying to repair a lot of damage and apparently bringing me on this visit will show that he's sincere in his efforts to get along better.'

She lay on the bed and Flo checked her impressive bump. 'You really are all baby.' The size was spot on, plus there was lots of movement. 'He's wide awake!' Flo laughed as the baby gave her hand a little kick.

He was head down and engaged, Flo told her, and then examined Maggie further.

'All seems quiet,' Flo said, and explained that there was no sign of the cervix thinning. 'For some women it happens over days and weeks, with some it happens in hours.'

Maggie gave an impatient sigh.

'You can still stay home. Just because there's no sign that you're in pre-labour it doesn't mean it won't happen and you're certainly entitled to rest up and enjoy these last days or weeks at home.'

'I know. It's not that I don't want to go to Idihr today and to the hospital opening tomorrow, it's just…' Her voice trailed off but Flo could guess what was wrong.

'You just want to meet your baby.'

Maggie nodded. 'I think this trip today might take my mind off it.'

'Well, I think it's good that you're keeping busy, and also, if you can get as much work out of the way now, you won't be putting so much pressure on yourself after the baby comes.'

'I also feel terrible asking you to come here and then practically leaving you alone for the next two days.'

'I'm hardly slumming it,' Flo said.

It was true. There was a driver at her disposal if she wanted to go in to the city, and if she wanted some time in the *hammam* all she had to do was let Kumu know.

They chatted for a while but soon it was time for Maggie to get dressed and be made up for the trip to Idihr. Again Maggie, checked that Flo would be okay on her own. 'What will you do with yourself?'

'I might go for a wander,' Flo said. 'Or I might do something about the lack of Christmas in this place!'

Maggie laughed. 'Well, good luck finding decorations.'

Flo didn't need luck.

She had come with tinsel!

Back in her suite she set to work.

There was no hope of a tree so she wrapped it around a stunning vase that was in the corner of the lounge area and then set about wrapping the presents she had bought.

There was a knock at the door. She guessed it might be Kumu and gave a cheery, 'Come in!'

It was Hazin.

Hazin looked exquisite. He was wearing a pale gold robe with buttons that ran the length of the front and he wore a *keffiyeh*.

Flo had only ever seen Hazin in a suit. She was so surprised to see him—and so taken aback by this exotic side to his beauty—that she didn't even say hi, just sat there, with her lost voice, holding the little outfit she had bought for the baby.

'How are you?' he asked.

'I thought you were Kumu.'

'She needs to shave, then.'

She laughed, but midway it faltered as she remembered how he had blanked her yesterday and how she had been determined to ignore him. Yet now, on closer inspection, she could see the tension in his features and guessed that he hadn't dropped by idly.

Hazin could see her sudden wariness. 'May I still come in?' he asked.

'Of course you may,' Flo said, and sighed at her complete inability to sulk around Hazin or play hard to get.

But games were not needed here, for he had come to apologise.

'I just wanted to say that I'm sorry I was rude to you yesterday,' Hazin said, and closed the door behind him.

Flo was rather unused to such a direct apology—in fact, she couldn't remember receiving such a sincere one before. 'It's okay. I guess it must have been a bit of a shock, seeing me here.'

'No, Ilyas had already told me that you were here when you were leaving to go into the desert.'

That surprised her.

Hazin came and sat down on the floor where she was wrapping up her presents.

'You're wearing a robe,' he said, and smiled. 'It suits you.'

'It's Maggie's,' Flo admitted. 'I might go to the souks and get some of my own as it feels a bit odd wearing her clothes. It didn't used to. We used to borrow each other's clothes all the time.'

'So why is it awkward now?'

'I keep waiting for her to change.' Flo sighed. 'It's nothing to do with her and all to do with me. I'm just worried that we're going to grow apart.'

'Have you spoken to her about it?' Hazin asked.

'I'm not very good at that sort of thing. I don't like making waves.'

'Flo tends to go with the flow.'

'I do.' She sighed. 'Wherever it leads.'

And in the case of Hazin it had led straight to bed.

She met his eyes and they just looked at each other for a long time.

'I'm sorry I was rude,' he said again.

'Apology accepted,' Flo said, and did not look away.

His scent was intoxicating and she liked him unshaved, as he was now. She could not help but wonder how rough his kiss would be, and she tried to haul herself back from such thoughts.

But she didn't try very hard.

There was an elemental want that danced between them and there was desire that ran like a cord, one that should have tightened and drawn them together, except he remained upright and out of reach.

She did not move closer, yet she begged for a kiss with her eyes and it seemed to her that he was feeling the same inexorable pull, yet it was he who broke eye contact. He looked down at the little rattle and all the presents she had shoved in her case.

'What's this?' he asked, and picked up the ladybird.

Flo battled with disappointment for she had been certain a kiss was just a breath away, but she tried to keep it from her voice as she answered his question. 'A rattle.'

He gave it a little shake. 'Won't he be too young to be into music?'

'It's not a maraca.' Flo laughed but then it faded. She couldn't really believe that he didn't know what toys were for. 'Well, I guess it could be for music, but really it's just a plaything.'

He was looking past her shoulder and Flo turned and followed his gaze to the vase she had decorated. 'It's tinsel.'

'That I had worked out.'

'I'm having Christmas withdrawal. I miss all the build-up...' Flo admitted. 'I'll ring my family on the day and we're going to have another Christmas when I get back home, but it's not the same. Mind you, last year was awful,' Flo said. 'I couldn't stand to admit to my family that I'd found out he was married. I was ashamed enough without all of them knowing.'

'So you pretended you were fine.'

Flo nodded. 'I didn't do a very good job of it, though. I forgot to put my stocking out...'

'Stocking?'

'You know!' Flo couldn't believe he hadn't heard of it. 'You practically grew up in England.'

'Ah, but I came back here on the Christmas breaks.'

'Well, on Christmas Eve you hang up a stocking at the end of the bed, and then when you wake up it's filled with presents and nuts and fruit.'

'Who fills it?'

'Father Christmas.'

Hazin frowned and she guessed that if he hadn't heard of Christmas stockings and thought a baby's rattle was a musical instrument then some further explaining might be required.

'Some people call him Santa.'

But she had misread his confusion for it was entirely aimed at her.

'Flo, I have heard of Santa. Please tell me you don't believe in him.'

'Of course not,' Flo said, 'but there is a certain magic to Christmas.'

'So who fills it up?' he persisted.

'Stop it,' she said.

'Oh, so it's a magical stocking that you put at the end of your bed?' he teased.

'Of course not. It's my mum who fills it.'

He blinked.

'While I'm sleeping, though I don't tell her that I know it's her...'

'You live with your parents?'

'No, but I go home for Christmas.'

'And you're telling me that at the age of...' He waited and she reluctantly gave her age.

'Twenty-nine.'

'At the age of twenty-nine your mother creeps into your bedroom and pretends to be Santa while you pretend that you don't know it's her...'

'Pretty much.' Flo nodded.

'How bizarre.'

'It's actually very lovely,' Flo said, and then she sighed. 'I was so excited to come here, and I still am, but I really am missing Christmas.'

'It hasn't happened yet.' Hazin pointed out.

'And it won't—Maggie's never really been into it. I think because it stirs up memories of her mum. I just love it, though.'

She told him about the other traditions her family kept up, which right now she missed, like presents under the tree and the decorations. 'On Christmas Eve Mum lights these redcurrant candles and she makes this gorgeous mulled wine with a little sachet of spices. It's my favourite scent in the whole world,' Flo said, but then she flicked her eyes away at the sound of her own lie, for she had a new favourite scent.

Hazin.

Raw and masculine with crisp fresh notes. If she could bottle him she would and dab it on each day.

Yet it did not come just from a bottle, for she had tasted his skin and even now she could recall that taste. She moved her gaze back to his and the note of lust in the air was back and she swore he could sense it too.

He looked down at her mouth and then back to her eyes. A kiss was as inevitable as the night they'd first met—though perhaps she was imagining it, for Hazin spoke on as if the air did not thrum with lust and as if they were not alone in her bedroom.

'What else will you miss?' Hazin asked.

Flo had to peel sex from her mind like a reluctant stamp and attempt to remember what they were discussing.

'I'll miss Christmas dinner.'

'I remember at boarding school they would serve it to us on the last day of term. I tried it once...' He pulled a face. 'I cannot see how you could miss that.'

'My mum makes an amazing one. I was just telling Maggie that she's going to freeze it for me.' Flo gave a small shrug. She was tired of talking about a Christmas that wasn't and so she asked about him. 'What's it like for you, being home?'

'I had dinner with Petra's parents last night.'

'How was it?'

'It went better than expected,'

Hazin had been so filled with dread yet their warm welcome had touched him.

His brother and the elders had thought that some sort of public acknowledgement of his rather reckless behaviour was required.

Hazin thought not.

He had privately apologised to her family for any pain his indiscretions had caused them, and he felt this was a far more appropriate gesture.

'They were as lovely as she was. I care for them very much.'

He looked so intently at Flo that she felt as if she was missing something, but then the moment was gone.

'What else have you done?' she asked.

'My parents have lectured me at length. Prior to that it was Mahmoud, the King's vizier, and no doubt later I'll be talked down to by my brother.'

'Talked down to?'

'No one thinks I am capable of writing a speech. They all want to check it first and are annoyed that I won't let them.'

'Have you written it yet?' Flo asked, and she was surprised that he laughed.

'No.'

His laughter had been at her perception but then it faded because writing this speech had been hanging over his head for weeks.

'Why don't you just speak from your heart on the day?' Flo suggested.

'The day is tomorrow,' Hazin said.

Flo could see he was almost grey, just at the thought of it. 'So, just say what feels right at the time.'

'We don't speak off the cuff here in Zayrinia.'

'I thought things were changing.'

Oh, they were, they were, Hazin thought, for he ached to take her to bed. He ached for the feeling her mouth gave on his and the company and comfort she brought him. Yet he knew he must wait and so he rolled his eyes and spoke of his brother instead.

'I'm glad that Ilyas is away today. He's so staid...'

'Ilyas is gorgeous,' Flo refuted. 'He's not staid at all.' Then she smiled. 'Maybe a tiny bit.'

It was like sharing a little secret.

'All my family do when I am here is complain to me about me. Then they wonder why I don't like coming back.' He looked at her. 'This time, though, there was a rather compelling reason.'

'The speech?' Flo said.

'No, the midwife.'

His flirtation was very direct and it swept through her like relief, even if she didn't believe him. 'You didn't come back here for me.'

'But I did.'

He should not be here, Hazin knew, for he couldn't help himself when he was around her, and he had to fight to resist reaching out for Flo with each and every breath he took.

No, he should not be here, yet here was exactly where he wanted to be. Hazin looked down at the presents she was wrapping and the little mint-green suit with an odd face embroidered on the front.

'Is that a dog?' Hazin asked.

'It's a dog with rabbit tendencies, I think. I just thought it was so cute that I had to buy it.'

'You like babies a lot.'

'Far, far too much.' Flo sighed. 'You'd think I'd get my fill at work...' She shook her head. Really! She was hardly going to tell Hazin just how much she would love her own baby—Flo had learned many times over that it wasn't the best flirting technique!

Yet Hazin seemed unfazed.

'The carpenter's door is broken,' he concluded, and when she gaped at his odd choice of words Hazin better explained. 'It is an Arabic saying. It means that you rush around taking care of others while neglecting your own needs.'

'I don't neglect them,' Flo said. 'I just…well, you don't just go out to the shops to get one.'

'No.'

'But, yes, the carpenter's door, while not broken, is very squeaky.' She started to laugh as she decided she liked his saying better than thinking of her ovaries as some ticking clock.

'I thought you would be with Maggie today,' Hazin said, but Flo shook her head.

'No.'

'Aren't you supposed to be watching her?'

'She's not going to suddenly pop!' Flo laughed, although Maggie's water could break at any minute! She very much hoped not, though she chose not to air *that* concern with Hazin. 'I'm sure if anything *starts* to happen then Ilyas will get her back home. First babies usually take ages.'

'Oh.'

'And she's not ready yet.'

'How do you know?' Hazin asked.

'You don't want to know.'

He pulled a face. 'I like how babies get in there, not how they come out.'

'I had rather worked that out, Hazin.'

She just had not worked *him* out for, despite the thrumming between them, he made not a single move and Flo was too wary to make one of her own.

'So, what are you going to do with your day?' he asked.

'I thought I might wander,' Flo said. 'I have to speak to Kumu and work out where I can go, but I wouldn't mind a day exploring. What about you?'

'I have to work on my speech.'

'Can I help?'

He gave a wry laugh that Flo could not interpret. She could not possibly know that she was, in fact, the problem, and yet, *here*, with her, was where he wanted to be.

A day with just them was completely irresistible. Like wagging school instead of buckling down to work on his speech.

And as he sat there, he remembered something, a long-ago day when no one had shown up in the nursery and his brother had come to the door.

He had been so surprised to see him. Hazin could absolutely recall the feel of the smile that had split his face at the unexpected sight of Ilyas unaccompanied by an elder.

But then the memory faded and he shook his head, trying to recapture it. They had gone exploring together.

'Come on,' Hazin said suddenly.

'Where?'

He didn't tell her.

Hazin didn't have to.

Like an eager Labrador, when he stood up so too did she.

Had there been a lead she'd have rushed off to grab it! She reminded herself she had to be more aloof, more restrained, less available.

Except her heart was already utterly available to him.

CHAPTER TWELVE

THEY WALKED ALONG a corridor she had not been down before. It was dark and, unlike most of the palace, dimly lit. In fact, the only light came from a small arched window at the end of it.

'This was the nursery,' Hazin explained, and pushed open a huge unguarded door. 'Of course, it is not used now.'

Flo rather hoped it wouldn't be used anytime soon! Unlike the rest of the palace, which was lush and oozed luxury, this room was incredibly dour.

'Is this where you and Ilyas were…?' She didn't know what word to use. Housed? Kept? It was just so drab and gloomy.

'No, Ilyas was raised in the leaders' wing, but one day the elder did not come to school him…' He could remember it just a little clearer now. 'Ilyas came and fetched me.'

He pushed open a heavy wooden door and, having experienced the trip from Maggie's suite before, when she saw the steps leading downwards Flo knew that it led to the *hammam* beneath the palace.

'Are we going swimming?' Flo asked.

'No, we're going exploring,' Hazin said as he led the way, determined that they would not be getting naked.

They passed under a low archway and through decorated tunnels but he took her beyond anywhere that Flo had been with Maggie.

'Down there is Ilyas's private area...' Hazin pointed, but as Flo went to head down he called her back. 'We can't go there.'

'Why? He'll never know, he's not here today.'

'We just can't.' Hazin said and then smiled at her ease at breaking the rules.

'Do you have your own area?'

'Not really.' He shook his head. 'I declined.'

Flo frowned, unsure what he meant, but Hazin was already heading in a different direction.

'We came down here.'

'Who?'

'Ilyas and I.'

He was starting to remember a time so long ago and so buried that Hazin had until now completely forgotten its existence.

'Come on,' he said as they walked further down natural stairways until they came to a low tunnel that they had to stoop to go through.

It was worth it, though.

They came out to a huge cave pool surrounded by the soft sounds of fountains. They were no longer plunged in darkness for it was dimly lit by a natural window in the cave that looked to the desert sky.

'I can remember coming here...' Hazin said, looking up. 'Ilyas and I, we were children...'

There hadn't been a single good memory of his childhood, not one.

Yet as he looked at the huge cave he remembered them as children. 'We came exploring.'

'Here?'

'I'm sure it was here.' Hazin nodded. 'But it was far lighter. It seemed to glow. We swam and then we sat over there.' Hazin pointed. It was all coming back to him. 'And I told Ilyas that I wished he was King.'

Hazin could remember that feeling exactly—the absolute assuredness and trust that he'd had in his older brother then.

'He was always sensible. That day, even before we headed off, he stopped and got food and drinks. I was annoyed at the time because I wanted to head straight off...'

'Then you were hungry after your swim.' Flo laughed.

'Yes.' Hazin nodded. 'It was such a good day.'

'How old were you?'

'I don't know. Little. We had an amazing day but when we got back to the Palace it went back to being the same. I hardly saw him.'

'How come?'

'He lived in a different part of the Palace. I have my own area. I was a lot of work for the nannies and it was soon decided I should be schooled overseas.'

'Why not here?'

'I was too rebellious,' Hazin said. 'They didn't want the people to know that.'

'So they sent you away?'

'Yes, and now they complain that I stay away. I cannot stand the way my father rules. He has no compassion for his people.'

'Ilyas is changing that,' Flo said. 'He's the real leader now.'

She knew everything, Hazin realised.

He was not used to outsiders knowing Palace business, but he found that Flo knowing it did not unsettle him.

The world felt more open than the closed one he had grown up in.

'Could you give Ilyas a chance?' Flo asked. 'You trusted him once.'

'I trust him still,' Hazin said. 'I know he will do the right thing by the people. He wants me to have a more prominent role.'

'Do you want one?'

It was refreshing to be asked, but he could not answer yet.

'I'll tell you what I want, Flo. I want to get past tomorrow. I want the speech made and to get it right for Petra's family.'

'It will be,' Flo said. She looked at his taut features and wished she could melt the strain away. She wished, how she wished, that he would reach for her, that he would suggest they swim, so she might wrap herself naked around him.

Yet he made no move.

Hazin, the Playboy Prince, had, since their one torrid night, been a complete gentleman.

Flo just wished it wasn't so.

And then something lovely happened. Fingers of light that had been streaming into the cave spread as the sun became aligned with the window and they were bathed in light.

It was how he had experienced it all those years ago, when he'd come here with Ilyas.

'Shall we swim?' Flo said, oh-so-casually.

Hazin stared out at the pool and his memory recalled the perfect temperature of the water. He longed to shed his robe and take her in; for their legs to tangle beneath the water; to kiss her wet as he took her deep; to lose themselves in each other for a while.

'No,' Hazin said and stood. 'We ought to get back.'

He knew he had confused her, for he could feel the signals his body gave out. He was as turned on as she, yet he had sworn he would wait.

That he would do this right.

She walked ahead of him this time and he tried not to notice the single blonde curl that coiled on the nape of her neck.

And when she stooped to make her way back through the tunnel, he did all he could to ignore a bottom dressed in velvet waving inches from his face.

What the hell had he been thinking, bringing Flo down here?

And they were not out of the caves yet.

Flo did not wait for Hazin to follow her out. Instead, she walked ahead and tried to sort her head out, which was rather an impossible ask with his footsteps behind her in this intimate, magical space.

'Not that way…' he called out to her when she turned to the right, but Flo ignored him, for she was intrigued.

There were huge white pillar candles lighting a passage and she saw that the tunnel was lined with red mosaic tiles.

'We're not allowed here,' Hazin told her.

'Since when did you care for the rules?' Flo said, and she looked at the softly lit tunnel. 'Who lights the candles?'

'The *hammam* maids do. Each candle burns for seven days and seven nights.'

'Is this Ilyas's area?'

'No,' Hazin said. 'Well, sort of. This leads to where his harem used to be housed.'

She was right, he did not care for the rules, so he took Flo by the hand and they walked down a long red tunnel until they reached a boudoir.

'This was his harem.' Hazin explained. 'That tunnel over there leads to Ilyas's area of the *hammam*.'

'We came in through the back door?'

'So to speak.' Hazin nodded. 'Only those summoned by Ilyas can go through there.'

Flo felt her cheeks go pink.

There wasn't much that made her blush, but for some reason that this had once been a harem did.

She looked around at the plump velvet cushions where they must have lain, awaiting his summons. There were many mirrors and glass bottles. Flo took the stopper off one and inhaled.

It was the most sensual space she had ever been in.

'Would Ilyas come in here and choose?'

'No,' Hazin said. 'This space was for them.'

Hazin watched as Flo pulled out silk scarves and tassels from the chests that lined the walls. Her curiosity had been aroused and he ached in his groin.

'The harem was disbanded when Ilyas announced he was to marry...'

'I would hope so!' Flo said, and she draped a scarf over her shoulders as if playing dress-up. 'Was yours disbanded too?'

'I never had one.'

'Oh, I guess you were too young,' Flo said as she draped herself over some cushions.

He frowned. 'I told you, I declined.'

She looked at him. Hazin fascinated her, he truly did. 'Why?'

He gave her a smile as he answered, a smile that simultaneously warmed her as it sent a little shiver of energy through her. 'I like the thrill of the chase, Flo—or at least I used to.'

'Used to?'

'People know who I am now so they tend to chase me.'

No wonder he had been so upset when he had thought she had been targeting him simply because she'd known his title. 'Hazin, I came over and spoke to you so that you'd stay long enough for Maggie to arrive. I didn't really think it was my place to break the news of her pregnancy to you.'

'I know that now.'

He stood looking around the luxurious space where Ilyas's harem had awaited his summons, then smiled at Flo, who was draping the scarf over her face.

'It's sexy isn't it?' she said.

'I guess, but there would certainly be no chasing required here. The only thing you need to pull is this.' He reached up and pulled a thick velvet rope and the bells in the centre rang out.

'Ooh,' Flo said, and got up and danced towards him. 'How do you want me, master?'

He laughed, but then the mood changed all of a sudden. He wanted her so much, and as she shimmied over to him he felt the pull of his eyes but then, when she neared him, he gave her a slight push of his hands instead of an embrace.

'Let's go back,' Hazin said, wishing she would leave it there.

Flo could not, though.

'I couldn't make more of a fool of myself if I tried,' she said, stinging at his rejection of her all over again.

'It's not that, Flo. I didn't bring anything.'

But she just stared back at him through narrowed,

hurt eyes. 'Excuses, excuses,' she said. 'A simple no will suffice.' She turned to walk off, embarrassed and cross with herself, for she had sworn that he would make the first move. And confused too, so confused, for she had been so certain of their mutual want.

'Flo.' He caught her wrist and turned her around. He loathed the look of shame he had caused on her face. 'It is not that I don't want you…' He could not explain, because Hazin had promised himself that he would not speak of his feelings for her until Petra's memory had been laid to rest. His rejection of her had been unintentionally cruel, and he didn't know how to make it right without breaking his promise.

How did he explain that if he touched her he might crack and reveal all that was on his mind? 'I do want you but…' He could not reveal himself fully, but he tried to a little. 'I would not be a considerate lover. I have a lot on my mind…'

'I don't need cartwheels!' Flo cried. As her anger dimmed she could see the utter wretchedness in his eyes and the desire between them was almost palpable. She guessed he must feel guilt, yet she could not really fathom why. 'I know tomorrow is huge but it's not as if you've been celibate these past ten years.'

'No,' Hazin said. 'But I can't have sex with feeling today.'

For if he did, he might break apart.

'Then don't,' Flo said. She looked at his mouth and the set of his jaw and she felt his hand hot on her wrist. For him she would risk rejection again.

'As I said…' Flo smiled seductively. 'How do you want me, master?'

She saw the stretch of his lips and watched his Adam's apple dip and then rise. She dragged her eyes down to the buttons on his robe. Flo removed her hand from his grip and he did not reclaim it, as one by one she undid the buttons.

There was no question he wanted her, as she could see how hard he was through his sunnah trousers, and she felt a little dizzy with lust herself.

So she tasted his neck again—just the light brush of her lips and the tip of her tongue this time. It shot her back to the night when they *had* made love. Not at first, but later, when their eyes had locked and her soul had leapt and met his.

But this was just sex, she reminded herself. Yet as she moved her mouth lower and tongued his flat nipple, she heard his ragged breathing and knew she was just kidding herself, for this was more than pure need because there might never be a *them* again.

She kissed and licked across his flat, taut stomach and she nipped the dark snake of hair with her teeth before slipping him out to her full view.

On that morning when they had woken up together, just before it had all gone wrong, she remembered how it had been between them as she slid her tongue around his head and wetted him as she had wanted to then. Her hands slid up his thighs and she cupped his balls. She felt her knees press into the velvet cushion on which she knelt, and he moaned with craving as with her other hand she circled the base of his shaft and applied light pressure, her lips dusting the delicate skin in pure torture. Then she licked his long delicious length over and over as he fought not to guide her head, but then came the bliss of her lips closing over his heated tip.

Hazin sucked in his breath as she took him all the way in and his mind went blank.

He moaned with relief for she was not gentle or tender, her mouth was as hot and hungry as he needed it to be.

Flo had never been more into anyone. She tasted every delicious inch of him, and she could feel the fight in him not to thrust so she worked him faster with her hand.

She could feel her own sex heavy and wet as Hazin lost his desperate fight and put his hands on either side of her head to control the movement. He cursed in Arabic and then he warned her.

Flo knew it was coming.

She had felt the tight swell of him, and the salty rush came with a shout and it was so primal that even as she slid him from her mouth she felt herself coming.

She knelt back on her heels as the waves of her climax rocked her body. He looked down at her flushed face and right into her china-blue eyes as she swallowed.

'Come here,' Hazin groaned, and he hauled her up and held her against his body. Flo leant her head on his chest and breathed in the sexy scent of them, and for a moment his arms wrapped around her.

He was breathless, but for the first time in months it felt as if he could breathe. 'When I can,' he said, 'I will make things right by you.'

'I enjoyed it too, Hazin. It wasn't a favour.'

That hadn't been what he'd meant, but now was not the time to explain.

He and Flo had to be on hold for now.

Yet on the slow walk back through the caves to the palace they were holding hands. They came back through the wooden door to the stark old nursery.

'You go out first,' Hazin said, but not unkindly.

They were both dishevelled and it would be awkward indeed if anyone saw them like this. It was not said dismissively either, for he smoothed her hair and straightened her robe and did what he could to make her not look as if she'd just had sex.

'Good luck tomorrow,' Flo said. 'I mean that.'

'Thank you.'

He made her feel brave, because normally she put on a smile or made a little joke, but now she said what she felt she must. 'Promise me one thing?' she said, and he nodded. 'Don't leave this time without saying goodbye.'

It had hurt.

And he knew that.

'I won't.'

That promise, at least, he could give.

CHAPTER THIRTEEN

HAZIN FACED THE MORNING.

He had slept, and he awoke in that damned bed to the sound of his breakfast being brought into the lounge.

Usually he called down for it at his chosen time, but no doubt it had been sent to serve as a check that he was awake.

Well, he was.

He took his breakfast out on the balcony that looked out to the stunning city and, beyond, the ocean.

Ilyas's balcony faced the desert, but Hazin preferred this view. And on a day he had been dreading for such a long time, he actually smiled as he remembered how Petra had loved to sit out here.

It was nice to remember her with a smile. He hadn't been able to do that in all these years, but then the moment was broken when he heard a knock on his door. No doubt it was Ilyas to check he was on track for today.

Or Mahmoud to cast his beady eyes over his speech.

He could try, but Hazin had taken Flo's advice and decided that he would speak from the heart. He knew all the formal parts that he had to say, and as for the rest he still did not know.

But it was neither Mahmoud nor Ilyas, but Kumu.

'I have that number for you.'

Hazin blinked, He had not expected Kumu to be able to get the information he had asked for so soon.

And certainly, if she had, he had not expected her to give it to him today.

'Thank you,' Hazin said. 'And, Kumu—'

'You don't have to say,' she interrupted with a smile. 'I won't say anything, I never would.'

'Thank you.'

'If I can be any further help, please just ask.' She gave a small bow but as she turned to go she remembered a request from the Crown Prince. 'Ilyas has asked for a copy of the speech so it can be translated for his wife.'

'Ilyas will not be getting a copy of my speech,' Hazin said. 'He is quite capable of telling his wife what is said.' He watched a tiny smile play on Kumu's mouth but he did not want her to get into trouble on his behalf. 'If he gets annoyed, tell him to speak with me.'

'Ilyas always speaks kindly to me,' Kumu said.

He didn't know his brother. This was something Hazin knew, but he was constantly being surprised by the way Ilyas was changing things around the palace. And through those changes he was getting to know his brother.

It was clear that Ilyas loved his wife, and the atmosphere in the palace was so much lighter than it used to be.

Back when they had been boys, Hazin had said that he wished Ilyas was King.

He had trusted him then and he still did.

He always had.

As Kumu turned to go, he called her back. 'Kumu, wait there, please.' He went through to the study and opened up a drawer, taking out two slim packages.

'Please,' he said when he returned, 'take a seat.'

It was most irregular for a prince to invite one of the staff to take a seat in their apartment and he could see her confusion but she did as she was told.

'How old is Rami now?' He asked after her daughter.

'She is eleven.'

'Petra was so excited when you brought her in to visit her. You made her days so much brighter with the pregnancy and the baby...'

'I miss her so much,' Kumu admitted.

'I know, and so I have something for you.' He handed her a package. When she opened it, she saw it was a beautifully bound book that Petra had loved to read and sometimes Kumu had read to her.

Inside was a jewelled bookmark and he saw her fingers trace it.

'This is too much.'

Hazin had considered that, for he knew they must struggle to send their child to Zayrinia's best school. As he had wrapped the gift he had thought about Petra, for she had tried to give Kumu a necklace once and she had declined. 'She could never sell it,' Petra had later explained to Hazin, 'so that would make it a burden.'

He hadn't understood then, but he tried to now.

'I want you to have something that Petra loved and that is the bookmark. I would also like you to have this.'

She opened the envelope he gave her and tears fell from her eyes as she read that Rami had been offered a full scholarship at the prestigious Zayrinia school.

'How did you know?'

'Because I thought of Petra and this is what she would want for you.'

It was a nice start to the day he had dreaded. When

Kumu had left he looked down at the number she had brought him.

He was about to put it off when he thought of his own words…

I thought of Petra and this is what she would want for you.

Hazin made the call.

Flo made her way to the grand entrance hall to say goodbye to Maggie as they left for the ceremony.

Well, mainly to say goodbye to Maggie, but also in the hope of a glimpse of Hazin.

He wasn't there.

In fact, few of the staff were, for Ilyas had insisted that all who wanted to could attend the ceremony, and so most were there.

Yes, times were changing indeed.

'Hopefully, if Hazin does make it, he'll appear sober this time,' Ilyas said to Maggie, and headed off to find out what the hell was keeping his brother.

Maggie rolled her eyes. 'I don't know what Hazin is playing at. He won't let anyone see his speech and he's been holed up in his apartment all morning, receiving guests.'

'Who?'

'I don't know. I just know that I'll be really glad when today's over.'

'Are you sure you don't want me to come with you?'

'You keep telling me I'm not made of glass.' Maggie laughed and then she realised what was going on. 'You weren't asking to come to the ceremony for *me*, were you?'

'No,' Flo admitted.

'Flo…' Maggie's face worried. 'I love Hazin, I really do. He has always been an utter gentleman to me but—'

'I already know his reputation,' Flo cut in. 'Maggie, don't worry. I went into this with my eyes wide open. Or at least I thought I did.' Flo hadn't expected to find love.

'When you say you "went into this"…' Maggie closed her eyes. 'I'm too late with my warning, aren't I?'

'You were too late three months ago.'

'Oh, my God,' Maggie said, and she sort of laughed and groaned at the same time, but she was clearly concerned for her friend. 'I don't want you to get hurt.'

'I've a feeling it's a bit late for that, too.' Flo said. 'And the only person I'll have to blame is myself.'

She didn't even pretend that she wouldn't hurt when they ended. And end they surely must. Flo just hoped this time he would keep his word and say goodbye.

But it was Hazin who was hurting today, Flo was certain.

'I just wanted to be a friendly face in the crowd.'

'Liar,' Maggie said. 'You just want to hear it for yourself.'

'True, though I'll have no idea what's being said.'

'Well, given my due date is so close, I think I might need my midwife to accompany me after all…' And then she stopped speaking and looked up. Flo followed her gaze.

Hazin looked regal. Together and composed.

He wore a silver robe and over that a black *bisht* that was trimmed in silver. His *keffiyeh* was elaborately wrapped and tied with a thick silver cord.

The King came out then and barked something at him but Hazin did not answer, just made his way slowly down the steps.

He did not look at the portrait and he did not look

at Flo, he just made his way through the open doors to the first of the waiting cars.

'Can Flo travel with me?' Maggie asked Kumu.

'Flo will come with me,' Kumu said. 'I shall take care of her and should you need her, just give me a discreet wave.'

Maggie looked at Flo. 'I'm sorry, I tried...'

'I was hardly going to come in the car with you.' Flo smiled. 'And Kumu's right, if you need anything just let me know. I'm glad I'm here for you today.'

The official cars were waiting to move off, and Kumu took her to another that was, of course, not part of the procession. In fact, she and Kumu left first so they could be there before the Royals arrived.

They drove through streets lined with people all waiting to glimpse not just Hazin but the Crown Prince they held out so much hope for and also his very pregnant bride, who they were desperate for news of.

As they headed towards the hospital, a huge crowd of people began cheering and Flo could not quite believe the turnout.

'Princess Petra was very popular,' Kumu explained. 'When she and Hazin married she came down and met with the people. It was as if a breath of fresh air had breezed into the palace, for the Royals had always kept themselves separate until then. Unfortunately, that breath of fresh air did not last.'

Flo was surprised at how much Kumu was telling her, but guessed she must be feeling sad today and perhaps needed to share.

Kumu turned then and smiled. 'Now that Maggie is here, things are different again,' she said. 'Now the people see Ilyas smiling. Do you remember the cheers on their wedding day?'

'I do.' Flo laughed. 'I was standing right at the back of the ballroom and I still had to put my hands up to my ears.'

It was so sad that Petra had died, and maybe Flo was torturing herself by going today, but it would be torture too, to stay away.

Once they had arrived, Kumu went to greet the Royal cars and Flo stood with the caterers and maids and security and the many people who were there to ensure that things went seamlessly.

The Royals would be seated on a covered platform. There was a lectern and beside that a beautiful image of Petra, and the platform was dressed in gorgeous desert blooms. There were rugs on their seats for the air was cool. That had actually been Flo's suggestion to Kumu and it had nothing to do with the weather, more the very pregnant princess and those waters breaking on a very public stage!

She watched as Maggie took her place on the platform and she smiled as she saw that Maggie was the first to cover herself with a rug. And Ilyas, because he loved her and did not want her to stand out, did the same.

But not the Queen.

There wasn't an empathetic bone in her body, Flo thought, but then ate her own words because the Queen did the same then too.

Hazin did not.

He sat absolutely still, like a statue.

There were moments, though, when she felt closer to him than she ever had to anyone. She could tell him things, reveal things and be entirely herself.

They had moments of absolute connection.

Now was not one of those moments, for he looked so

alone up there on the platform. Not sad, or lonely, just separate from the people who surrounded him.

He did stand and smile as three more people came to the stage, presumably Petra's parents and brother. They all sat beside him and then the crowd hushed as the ceremony began.

It was all very formal. There was a band that played for *ever*, and a whole lot of speeches, and then the band played *again*.

And then Petra's brother made a speech and Flo watched as his mother dabbed at her eyes.

Not the Queen. She remained remote and untouched.

And then Flo held her breath as Hazin came to the lectern and the crowd hushed immediately. You could have heard a pin drop as everyone listened intently as their long-absent Prince, for the first time in a decade, made a speech.

He spoke in Arabic, so of course Flo had no idea what was said, but his voice was clear and only a couple of times did it become husky with emotion.

Flo stood, her teeth working her bottom lip, watching his pale features, the only real sign of how difficult this was for him. And then she straightened her features to appear more impassive as Kumu came and stood by her side.

'He just thanked all the medical staff and he said that this new facility is much deserved and needed.'

'I see.'

'And now he says that Petra's family draws a lot of comfort from this new facility.'

Flo nodded.

'Hazin says now how kind Petra was. He says he would like to reiterate that, for...' Kumu hesitated. 'She truly was.'

Kumu was crying, Flo realised.

'Now Hazin says that it has taken him a long time, but he understands that seeds of kindness were planted in him and that this is how she remains with him. For now, when he is angry, he tries to think of Petra, and what she would do. Hazin says that it is never too late to change…'

Flo watched as he turned briefly and looked back at the people behind him, and she wondered if he had looked directly at his parents as he spoke on.

'He says,' Kumu continued, 'that we can all learn from her. And even today he tries to follow her wise words. He hopes that today she smiles on all of us.' Kumu choked and then added, 'And him.'

The crowd applauded and then it built and built to a cheer. Flo could see how much the people loved him.

And so did she.

He had made the dreaded speech without notes and she knew that every word had come from his heart. Flo felt her heart twist with misplaced jealousy, for her rival was a ghost.

As the crowd's applause faded, he turned and guided Petra's mother to cut the ribbon and officially declare the facility open.

He was very patient with her, Flo thought, and watched as he steadied the emotional woman's arm with his hand as she cut the ribbon.

Hazin might have a scandalous reputation but, Flo knew, he really was a very nice man.

And she was more than a little in love with him.

Flo felt nothing like she had this time last year.

Then it had been about dressing up and going out and all the stupid superficial things.

With Hazin it was all the little things that mattered.

Finally it was over, yet perhaps not for Hazin. Flo watched as he mingled with the guests and duly made small talk as waiters milled around.

A sad garden party really, Flo thought.

Even Flo was not ignored. In fact, just before it was time to leave, Hazin made his way over to her. She decided to take a lesson from Perfect Petra and be…

Kind.

'Well done,' she said.

'Thanks.'

'It seemed to go very well.'

'I think so.'

She didn't know what to say, for there was a stretch of awkward silence so Flo filled it.

'I know that you must miss her so much.'

'Please…' He took a breath for he could not deal with it today. It *had* to be later. Hazin's eyes shuttered as he braced himself to get through the rest of this most difficult day. 'Not now, Flo!'

His words came out too harshly, Hazin knew, and yet there was no chance to rectify things with the world watching.

And so he walked away.

CHAPTER FOURTEEN

IT WAS KUMU who brought Flo's breakfast in the next morning and it took more than a moment for Flo to register that it was Christmas Eve.

Not that it felt like it here in the desert kingdom.

'How did you sleep?' Kumu enquired as she placed the breakfast tray on Flo's lap.

'Very well,' Flo lied, and then asked a question. 'Kumu, have there been any deliveries for me?'

'If there were they would have been sent straight to your room. Is there anything you need that I can get for you?'

'No, I have everything.' Flo smiled. 'I just...' She held in her disappointed sigh. 'I thought my family might have sent something for Christmas.'

'I shall look into it myself,' Kumu said. 'If anything comes, it shall be delivered straight to your suite.'

'Thank you.'

'Flo, I know that we don't do Christmas here, but I wondered if, as a treat, you might like to sleep in the western wing tonight. The view of the desert at sunset is spectacular.'

'It's lovely of you to offer...' Flo smiled '...but, no, thank you. I really like it where I am.'

'You're sure?' Kumu checked.

'Absolutely.'

It was madness, Flo knew, yet the first thing she had done when Kumu had opened the drapes had been to check for Hazin's plane.

She could read the insignia on the tails a lot better now and it soothed her to know that he was still here. Yes, he had promised not to leave without saying goodbye, but men would promise anything after a good blowjob.

And if that was crass, she was only being crass with herself, because distance from him made Flo bully herself. And that bully rearranged her thoughts until she had decided that she had thrown herself at him in the *hammam*.

And though they had both enjoyed it, there had been nothing since then bar that brief exchange after his speech. Flo picked at her breakfast and then cast her mind back to yesterday and the moment they had shared.

Not now, Flo!

She could still hear his words and feel the tension with which they had been delivered. Flo could kick herself for being insensitive and for saying what ten thousand people yesterday had surely already said to him.

From all Flo could gather, Hazin had not returned to the Palace last night.

Where had he spent the night?

Give it up, Flo told herself, and hauled herself from the bed.

Yet she could not let it go.

She had known from the start that he came with a warning attached.

Yet it wasn't his reputation or other women that concerned her.

It was Petra.

Flo, dressed in a soft, indigo velvet robe, stepped out onto the balcony and tried to shift her low mood. It was cold, though not, Flo thought, cold enough for it to be Christmas, not while the sky was so high and blue.

And his plane was still here.

Of course there were no decorations in the palace. Flo noted their absence as she made her way to Maggie's wing.

'Morning.' Maggie smiled and greeted her friend. 'Have you had breakfast?'

'I have.' Flo nodded as she wandered in and took a seat on one of the couches. Maggie came and sat with her and they gazed out at the stunning desert view. 'It feels odd not to be hitting the shops today,' Flo admitted. Usually she was the last of the last-minute Christmas shoppers but had made sure that she'd got it all done before she'd left. 'It doesn't feel like Christmas at all.'

'I feel bad that I've let it slide.'

'Well, you've been pretty busy.' Flo shrugged. 'I'm just a Christmas tragic.'

'And this is going to be your worst.'

'No.' Flo shook her head. She didn't want Maggie feeling guilty. 'I'm having the most amazing time and I am so glad that I came. It was *last* Christmas that was the worst ever.'

'Oh, that's right, while I was away you broke up with…?' Maggie frowned. 'I can't remember his name.'

Flo smiled at her friend's irritation with her own brain.

'What was his name?' Maggie said, clicking her fingers in exasperation, as if that might make his name suddenly appear.

Flo decided it was time to share with Maggie his rightful description—and it was far worse than one that began in B and ended in D. 'His name was Married Man.'

'Oh, Flo.' Maggie put her arms around her friend. 'Why didn't you say?'

'Because I was just so ashamed. His wife came in to have her baby…'

'You poor, poor thing.' Maggie was completely lovely. 'You could have told me.'

'I know, I just didn't know how.'

It was since she'd told Hazin that she'd felt if not better then a little less brushed by the shame. 'I do know how to pick them, don't I?'

'You really, really do.' Maggie sighed and then told Flo what little she knew about Hazin. 'Apparently he came back very late last night and left early this morning.'

'Do you know where to?'

'I don't,' Maggie said, and then her voice was serious. 'Though he's asked to speak formally with Ilyas tonight. Ilyas seems to think that now Hazin has got the speech out of the way he's going to formally request to step down.'

'And how does Ilyas feel about that?'

'He wants Hazin beside him.'

'Don't we all,' Flo said, and then buried her face in her hands. 'I'm sorry, Maggie, my disaster of a love life is the last thing you need to hear about right now.'

'It's exactly what I need,' Maggie said. 'I've missed you so much, you know.'

Maybe she could address it? Flo thought of Hazin's

suggestion to talk about what was on her mind. But Flo did not want to heap pressure on Maggie now and tell her her insecurities about the future of their friendship. So instead she did what she did best—shook off her mood and pushed out a smile.

'I'll be fine.'

'Better than fine,' Maggie said. 'I've told the *hammam* to expect us this afternoon! I think we could both use a spa day.'

It was a very different Christmas Eve indeed.

Flo left Maggie and met with two nursery nurses who would be helping once the baby was here. She also spoke with the palace elder who went through a few details about what was required after the birth had taken place.

'There are already people gathering and watching activity at the palace. It is one of the reasons that we prefer the birth to take place here. It allows the family some time before it is announced to the world.'

'How long before it is?'

'That is a choice for the parents. For Ilyas it was two weeks after his birth and for Hazin I believe it was a couple of months.'

'A couple of months?'

'The baby is brought onto the balcony, or that is what used to happen. Ilyas says that the announcement shall be made on the day the baby is born but the balcony presentation can come afterwards, whenever Maggie is ready.'

Flo could more than see the merit of giving birth here without the world waiting impatiently to hear the news. Maggie was shielded from a lot of what was happening, for certainly Flo would not be telling her about the crowd already gathered. It really sounded as if Ilyas had done all he could to ensure his wife was well looked after.

And that included having Flo here.

After lunch, she and Maggie made their way down to the *hammam*, but Maggie could not relax at the foot massage. She was just as tense through all the gorgeous treatments so Flo suggested they go into one of the pools.

The water was bliss and just the right temperature. Maggie lay on her back as Flo leant over the edge and stared out at the desert.

It was late afternoon and in a couple of hours the sun would be setting. Flo could have accepted Kumu's kind offer and had that view all to herself.

Yet she had placed herself on Hazin-watch, furtively checking for his plane and all too aware that at any moment he could leave. It sounded as if he would tonight.

He was surely stepping down.

Why else would he want to see Ilyas?

And it made her sad.

There was a guilty shard in her soul that relished the thought of him living in London and the chance it might give them, but mostly she was sad.

She didn't blame him for turning his back on his parents, who had treated him so abysmally, but the people all loved him so much, that was clear to Flo. And, despite his rather staid exterior, Ilyas wanted to right the wrongs that had been done to them and to have a relationship with his brother. Yet Hazin pushed away anyone who attempted to get close to him, that was abundantly clear.

And so she would close her drapes on the view tonight and stop watching for planes leaving and searching for signs.

She had a job to do.

Maggie was in pre-labour, Flo was quite certain, for she was irritable and unable to relax, though the water seemed to be doing the trick now for there was a lovely feeling of calm.

Flo was on Maggie-watch now.

CHAPTER FIFTEEN

IT WAS A very quiet Christmas Eve indeed.

Tired from the massages and time in the pool, Maggie was early to bed and Flo lay in hers with the drapes firmly closed. If she was right and Maggie was in early labour, at any time her phone could go off so Flo was more than happy to have an early night. But first she called home.

'Flo, I can't talk for long,' her mother warned, which wasn't exactly a great conversation starter. 'I have so much to do.'

'Tell me,' Flo said, desperate to be a part of the celebrations, but her mother didn't have time to indulge her suddenly homesick daughter. And so Flo lay on her bed watching a Christmas movie on her computer and eating chocolate.

It would be perfect, really, if it wasn't Christmas Eve.

And if she wasn't bracing herself for a broken heart.

She was all floppy and tired from her spa and she frowned when there was a knock at her door. But as she pulled on a wrap Flo was sure it was Kumu to tell her to come and see Maggie.

It was Hazin.

'What do you want?' she asked, and her voice was all surly, for she refused, yes, *refused* to jump to his tune.

'I want you to come to bed,' he said.

'Excuse me?' Flo checked, not sure if she was hearing things right. It would seem that she was! 'Hazin, what happened to the thrill of the chase?'

'You're easy, though,' he teased, and then saw her murderous expression and quickly amended with a slight triumphant smile, 'Flo, I prefer the thrill of you.'

He melted her.

Her resolve popped in the same way she'd feared Maggie's waters would until it lay in a puddle on the floor. Still, she did *try* to resist him, even if he had just made her smile.

'I'm not your sex toy, Hazin. Anyway, I need to sleep.' She went to close the door but his shoulder got in the way.

'Sleep in my bed, Goldilocks.'

'Ha-ha.'

'We've managed to just sleep before,' Hazin pointed out. In fact, it rather suited him *not* to have sex tonight, for he desperately wanted the air cleared between them before they did. He was holding onto a secret indeed. 'You have to come to my apartment, I've got a surprise there for you.'

Flo was intrigued.

And she wanted to know what had been said between him and Ilyas, not that she could admit she knew he had just been in a meeting.

'Bring your phone,' he said. 'You may be gone some time.'

She really was a pushover where Hazin was concerned, Flo thought as she quickly pulled on her robe and happily collected her phone.

Down long corridors they went and then they entered his apartment.

He led her towards his bedroom and as she opened the door to darkness, there was a familiar scent in the air. It wasn't pitch dark, for there was a candle burning and he handed her a glass of warm mulled wine.

'It's a redcurrant candle,' Flo said shaking her head in wonder, because it most certainly was.

'Happy Christmas Eve,' Hazin said.

'This is the nicest thing you could have done.' Flo beamed. She was very close to tears, for she could not quite believe what he had done! There was one problem, though. 'I can't have a drink tonight,' Flo said, and told him the real reason she had to sneak in some sleep. 'I've a feeling I'm going to be needed by Maggie.'

'Really?' He thought for a moment. 'Well, you can have some tomorrow then.'

He took the glass from her and put it down and then turned on the side lights as she breathed in the lovely scent of a Christmas at home. Well, minus the pine and the mince pies and things, but quite simply he had taken her breath away.

'Thank you for this, Hazin!'

'You are so welcome.'

'I was starting to feel a bit homesick.'

'Then come here,' he said, and lay on the bed. A moment later she had joined him. It was bliss to be in his arms and just to lie and chat and be held. 'Do you really think Maggie will have the baby tonight?' he asked.

'Well, it's not an exact science, but I think things are starting to move along.'

'How come?'

'She's distracted, a bit irritable...' Flo couldn't really explain it. 'I haven't said anything to Maggie, of course. You just get a feeling about it, I guess, though I may well be wrong and I shall have foregone my mulled wine for no reason.'

'There's plenty whenever you're ready.'

'So you're going to stick around?' Flo asked, not so subtly fishing for information.

'I think so,' Hazin said. 'I just spoke with Ilyas.'

'And?' Flo asked.

'I don't want to talk about it now,' Hazin said.

In many ways she was happy not to hear his decision just yet.

Whatever he had chosen, it would hurt.

Still, there was a part of her that simply wanted more information.

'If you're ever back in London...'

'Flo...' He warned that the subject was closed.

'I'm just saying we might bump into each other.'

'Like we did the first night, when you just *happened* to be at Dion's?'

Flo smiled. 'No, maybe on the tube...'

'I think we did cross paths once.'

'Really?'

'I'm sure it was you. It was winter and I specifically remember you were wearing jeans and boots...'

It took a second to realise she was being teased because half the women in London would have been wearing jeans and boots in winter.

Still, Flo smiled at the thought that their paths might have crossed one day and accepted that the subject of his chosen future was closed. And so she asked him another question instead. 'Are you looking forward to being an uncle?'

'I don't know. I've never had anything to do with babies.' He thought for a moment. 'Ilyas seems happy, though.'

'He does.'

'And the mood at the palace has certainly improved since the last time I was here. It's nothing like it used to be.'

'What was it like when you came home at Christmas from school?' Flo asked.

'Well, it wasn't Christmas, for one thing.'

'But what was it like?'

She wanted to know.

'I had nannies when I was younger and then from the age of about eleven I took care of myself. Really, I didn't see anyone when I was here in the holidays, unless there was an official function. Ilyas was housed in the leaders' wing or taken out to the desert and immersed in the teachings.'

'Did you eat together?'

'No,' he said. 'Well, we did on formal occasions.'

'So where did you eat?'

'I was served my meals in the dining room here.'

'In the apartment?' Flo said, and she swallowed and thought of a child virtually alone in this huge space.

You really can have everything and nothing, Flo thought.

'I loathed coming home,' Hazin admitted, and he gave her arm a squeeze. 'But not this time.'

'I'm glad I've entertained—'

'You're not the entertainment, Flo,' Hazin said, and he meant it. So much so that it was then that he remembered she might soon have to work. 'Let's get some sleep.'

They undressed and slipped into bed. He turned off the lights so that all that lit the room was the scented candle.

He lay on his back with Flo curled up into him, her

head on his chest. He smelt heavenly and the feel of his naked stomach beneath her fingers had her wonder if she might just have to change her mind about sex.

He was so unexpectedly romantic this evening.

But she must not get ahead of herself.

As nice as tonight had been, it was a glass of mulled wine and a candle.

Yet it was the little things he did that made her heart glow, and she could not help but hope that there was more to come, for he had made this night away from home so special.

She had assumed, right up to now, that the gesture had been a bit of a ruse to get her into bed.

Not that he had needed a ruse.

Yet Hazin didn't seem to mind a bit that she needed to sleep.

But now she wanted a kiss.

Except Hazin really was asleep!

Not just asleep—his breathing had gone from deep to a gentle snore.

Flo lay there smiling as the noise from her less-than-perfect Prince grew louder.

'Hazin,' she said, and gave him a little prod.

It didn't do the trick.

'Hazin!' she said louder, and this time he got a kick.

He awoke a little and disengaged her from his arms, then rolled onto his side so they faced each other. They shared a smile. 'I don't usually snore,' Hazin said.

'Liar.'

'I don't, I'm just wrecked.'

These last few days had been busy. Racing around to get things done and seeing Petra's family, followed by the drain of relief at having given the speech.

And the guilt.

For Hazin had been busy making plans.

But he did not want to examine guilt now, for rather than speak their mouths met in a sleepy kiss.

There was just a whisper of resistance in him, for he wanted a clean slate, a clear head before he lost himself, but that whisper faded in the melding of their mouths.

Softly and slowly Hazin kissed her, his large hand lightly stroking her bare arm.

His calf came over her and she felt its heavy weight hook her in as they drank the intoxicating lust from each other's mouths.

Hazin's hand moved from her arm and stroked her waist, shooting arrows of desire to her centre. It was such an unhurried kiss yet it was the most sensual of her life.

Hazin had not brought her to his bed for this, yet there was no thought process now, just the sensation of being lost in a kiss.

Sometimes it had felt as if they'd been playing a game of cat and mouse, but not now.

Desire wrapped them closer. She opened her eyes to his and his gaze awaited her, and suddenly Flo remembered the first night they had met.

That moment when their souls had locked had felt the same as this, only this was deeper and this time they did not hide from it, or look away.

She was burning at his kiss and his touch, wrapped so tightly in his embrace. Flo freed her leg so that she could move it over his thigh, thus opening herself to him, for she had to have him inside, right now.

Her hand stretched down and felt him, hard and strong and ready. Hazin's hand encircled hers, and together they stroked him until they could bear it no longer. She guided him there but one of them at least was sensible, and his hand released hers as he went to reach for a condom.

'I'm on the Pill, Hazin.'

Those were words Flo had never said before, but to break contact now would feel criminal.

They were words that Hazin had always ignored.
Until now.

Hazin entered her slowly, relishing the feel of her tight, warm grip and he swallowed her sigh of pleasure.

Utter pleasure as he stretched her completely and their mouths met again. There was a delicious daze at his tenderness as they moved together, slow and unhurried.

Those strong arms were Flo's to explore tonight and she felt the silky skin that sheathed his muscles, while his tongue stroked hers in enticing circles. The heat they made could surely light the dark desert sky.

He rolled her onto her back and kissed her in a way Flo had not known existed until now. She found out first-hand how that rough, unshaven face felt when it rubbed against her soft skin.

He took her hands and held them over her head, their fingers laced.

Her legs wrapped around him and Flo arched into him. She knew, beyond a shadow of a doubt, that he was making love to her.

Hazin was drowning in the intimate embrace of her and he swallowed down the soft moans that came from her throat.

He freed her hands so she could explore his face, and he drew up on his hands so he could watch her and kiss her. He took her in rapid, measured thrusts that had her grit her jaw together at times and had her stretch up for a kiss at others.

Hazin took her harder, holding nothing back. He watched as she helplessly grasped at pillows to anchor herself, then give in to the absolute force of his thrust. He felt her climax gather and the zip of tension in her made his stomach lift.

The room felt like a vacuum that sucked the air from him as he shot into her. He released with a breathless shout, and *this* was how it should be, Hazin knew.

This, he thought as he felt her release beneath him and revelled in the softness of the air in the aftermath of lovemaking.

His eyes opened to darkness and there was a shiver of guilt that ran through Hazin for the love Petra had never known. The defences inside with which he had walled that regret were temporarily down and Hazin wished, how he wished, that she had known love. In the still of the night, his soul spoke and he voiced that regret out loud. 'Oh, Petra.'

Flo froze beneath him.

Lost to her orgasm, utterly gone, she was hauled back as her lover said his late wife's name while still inside her.

It was like being sluiced with filthy water.

Lost in bliss, about to float gently back to earth, she was instead hurtled into high alert and her eyes snapped open. There was no denying what she had heard and Flo shoved him off her.

'Flo…' he attempted, but she was already half way out of the bed. His hand reached for her and came down on her shoulder but she shrugged it off.

'Don't touch me!' she told him through tense white lips.

She could not believe what had just happened and

what she had just heard, but knew there could be no coming back from this.

She flicked on the light and then scrabbled on the floor, trying to find her robe, desperate to get out and feeling as if she might well throw up, when her phone rang.

Not now! Flo thought.

Please, please, not now.

But she looked at her phone and, yes, it clearly wasn't Flo's night for it was Maggie.

Flo couldn't even bear to sit on the bed as she took the call, she just turned her back on Hazin.

'Hey,' Flo said, and tried to keep her voice as upbeat as possible.

'Flo, I've been having contractions. I think the baby's close.'

Flo asked a few questions and told Maggie she would be along very soon. First, though, she had to have a shower.

'Is she having it?' Hazin asked. He was sitting on the edge of the bed with his head in his hands.

'What do you think?' Flo sneered.

'Can we speak for two minutes?'

'You don't get another moment of my time,' Flo said, and grabbing her clothes she headed into his bathroom and slammed the door behind her.

Flo was very used to quick showers but this was the quickest of her life.

She felt as if she had been beaten all over and she was desperate to cry but there was no time to.

Hazin tried to speak to her, though.

He went into the bathroom just as she was turning off the taps and stepping out.

'Please, Flo. Let me explain—'

'Don't even try,' she said as she dried off and dressed with lightning speed. 'I've been made to feel bad in my time, but what you just did to me…' She picked up his comb and quickly ran it through her hair. In the mirror she could see the redness of her face as she practically glowed with humiliation and pain. 'Why don't you go back to bed, Hazin, and get off to your late wife.'

It was nasty but, hell, it was merited and Hazin closed his eyes as she brushed past and walked out.

They were done.

CHAPTER SIXTEEN

FLO WALKED SWIFTLY through the Palace.

There was no IV cupboard to hide away in this time.

No other staff she could call on to cover for her.

There was the Palace doctor, of course, but she would never let down her friend.

She had to push aside what had happened.

It was hard to, though.

Flo wanted to pause and have a cry, or to catch her breath.

A few moments ago she had been in his arms, locked in bliss...

As Flo walked through the grand entrance towards the leaders' wing she ignored the portraits, yet it felt as if Petra's eyes were following her.

'Have him!' Flo said out loud, to the bemusement of two guards who stood at the foot of the stairs.

And with that small outburst she did what she could to let it go.

She would examine her pain later but right now she had Maggie to focus on.

Flo loved her job. As she climbed the staircase and entered the Royal wing that housed Maggie and Ilyas, she drew on that fact. This was about Maggie and being with her as she brought life into the world.

Flo put on a smile and walked into the Royal suite. Maggie was leaning against Ilyas and deep in the midst of a contraction.

Flo went over and felt the strength of the contraction. 'How long have you been having them?' Flo asked.

'Since Ilyas got back from seeing Hazin.'

'Maggie!' Ilyas said in slight reprimand and then addressed Flo. 'I think she started to have them when I was about to go and speak with my brother. I told her I could speak to Hazin at another time, but Maggie insisted she was fine.'

'So since around seven,' Flo checked, and Maggie nodded.

It was now just coming up for midnight.

Flo got Maggie up onto the bed and gave her a gentle exam to see how far along things were.

'Should we call the Palace doctor to come?' Ilyas asked.

'You can call if you would prefer to,' Flo said, 'but he'll be around for quite some time.' She smiled at Maggie. 'You're three centimetres dilated.'

'Three?' Maggie's voice was a touch incensed. 'That's it?'

'That's excellent,' Flo said, in positive midwife-speak, but Maggie didn't want to hear it!

'How can I only be three centimetres dilated?' As another contraction hit she started to moan. 'How bad is it going to be?'

'It's going to be absolutely fine,' Flo assured her.

Flo let the Palace doctor know what was happening and he came and checked on Maggie, but was very affable and understood her desire for as much privacy as possible during the first stage. Flo assured him she would call when things had moved along, or if she had any concerns in the interim.

Ilyas suggested that Maggie lie down for a while and try to relax, and when Maggie agreed Flo thought it best to leave them to it for now. There was an area outside the main bedroom, once used for maids and such, but tonight it served as Flo's staffroom.

She made a huge mug of tea and curled up in a chair, keeping her thoughts on Maggie, rather than dwelling on Hazin.

It was too hard to do both.

Her broken heart would be there waiting at the other end of the birth, so for now she pushed it aside and focused on Maggie and the baby soon to be born.

Maggie dozed between contractions and then had a bath, and as she climbed out her waters broke.

'I was so worried it would happen on the stage...'

'I know you were.' Flo smiled as she listened to the baby's heart rate. 'Your baby is behaving beautifully for you.'

The contractions strengthened and started coming closer together and when even the huge bedroom felt confined, they moved out onto the balcony as the dawn broke.

'What a beautiful day to have a baby,' Flo said.

A Christmas baby.

It *was* magic.

Somehow Christmas always was.

Even last year when she'd been so low, it had been a wonderful family day.

And on this one she would deliver her best friend's child.

Or the Palace doctor would.

But Flo got to do this part.

This lovely part where the world was all hushed as Maggie leant on the stone wall and tried to breathe through the pain. The contractions were coming close together now and Maggie was finding them overwhelming.

'You are doing so well,' Ilyas said in his deep voice.

He wasn't staid, Flo decided. In fact, he was incredibly stoic and calm and exactly what Maggie needed.

As Maggie groaned, Ilyas put his hand on the small of his wife's back and massaged her there as Flo had shown him, but now it did not appease her and she pushed his hand off.

'Go and get Flo her present,' Maggie said, and Ilyas frowned.

'Now?'

'Yes, now,' Maggie said, and her voice was urgent.

Flo knew things were moving along, just by her friend's need to set the world to rights.

'I thought you'd forgone Christmas,' Flo said.

'Not for you.'

And that touched her heart, because they were such good friends and while it wasn't a big deal to Maggie, it was to Flo. She smiled as Ilyas returned to the balcony with a beautifully wrapped gift.

'Open it,' Maggie ordered.

It was a *hammam* towel and a gorgeous glass bottle of oil that smelled the same as the one the maids had applied to her hair.

'They're gorgeous,' Flo said. 'Thank you so much.' But Maggie still wasn't appeased.

'Read the card!' Maggie shouted.

Flo loved a woman in transition!

The dominatrix effect, she jokingly called it, and gave Ilyas a smile.

But then, when she did as she was told and read her card, Flo felt tears well in her eyes.

Dear Flo,
Any time you need a spa day, know that I do too
and that the hammam *awaits. I still can't get used*
to being rich, but you can come here whenever
you want, even for a weekend.
We are best friends and we need our spa days,
Maggie xxx

Flo had wondered if things might change between them, and if Maggie being a princess might somehow be the end of their friendship. Over and over she had told herself it would not and had reminded herself that this was Maggie. Yet at times she had doubted and worried, and Maggie had clearly understood that she might.

It meant so much.

'Thank you,' Flo said. 'I shall be sure and use my gift often.'

'Well, make sure you do!' Maggie snarled, but then she wavered as her body took over. 'I want to push.'

'Then do.'

For an hour or so more it was still just the three of them. Maggie moved onto the bed and asked for darkness so Flo closed the drapes on the gorgeous day, and with just the sidelights they got down to the gritty end of birth.

Pushing was hard and exhausting work, but Maggie got the hang of it and real progress was being made.

'I'm going to call for the doctor,' Flo said, and as Ilyas encouraged his wife, Flo made the call and opened up the delivery pack.

'Another push,' Flo said. 'You are so close to meeting your baby, Maggie…' She looked up and smiled as the doctor and elder came in.

The elder was lovely and he went and sat where Flo had throughout the night drunk an awful lot of tea. The doctor too was charming and did not rush to take over.

It was just a gorgeous, natural birth and as Ilyas held Maggie's leg, Flo held the other and then hugged her friend through the very end of it as Ilyas watched his son being born.

He really was a beautiful baby.

Long-limbed and with a lusty cry, he was delivered onto Maggie's stomach and Ilyas cut the cord.

'I've got a son,' Maggie said, and though they had all already known that the baby would be a boy, it was wonderful to watch her friend's pure joy that her son was here.

Flo covered them in a blanket so the baby lay on his mother's chest, and his cries soon faded. He had a little feed, which helped with the delivery of the placenta.

And there was still no rush, there was plenty of skin-to-skin time before the doctor asked for him to be brought over so he could be checked.

He really was perfect. With huge dark blue eyes and thick black hair, he was the image of his father.

'Your son is very healthy,' the doctor said, and Flo wrapped the little man up and handed him to Ilyas.

Often, first-time fathers were awkward, but Ilyas was confident and held him close as he carried him over to Maggie.

It was a lovely family moment, so as the elder and doctor went to inform the King and Queen of the birth of their first grandchild, Flo stepped out onto the balcony to give them some time alone.

And for some time alone for herself too.

Now that the baby was safely here and the intensity of the past hours was fading, Flo could feel anew the hurt that had propelled her from Hazin's bed.

She closed her eyes on the bright mid-morning sun because tears were dangerously close.

She was thrilled for Maggie, absolutely so, yet Flo ached, she just ached because it felt like a knife was twisting in her gut at another appalling mistake made in the romance department.

Maybe she should be more like Maggie and be mistrusting of people. Instead, she was like that bloody eager Labrador, jumping whenever the master called.

No more.

She was through.

Of course, she would stay for the rest of her leave and she would return often, because there was no way she would let Hazin affect her friendship with Maggie. But as for Hazin she was done.

Flo was angry and hurt and felt cold to the bone.

But there was still work to be done so she pressed her fingers to her temples and took in a deep breath before heading back inside.

'Where's Ilyas?' Flo asked when she saw Maggie alone, holding the baby.

'He wanted to speak with his parents and not just leave it to the elder.'

'Do you think they'll come and see him?'

'I don't know,' Maggie admitted. 'I don't think they took any interest at all in their children, but things do seem better since we married.'

'Well, let me get you tidied up just in case,' Flo suggested.

It was all very seamless.

With no expense spared, the room had been very

well prepared for the Royal birth. Flo soon had all the equipment moved out, and the new mother sitting up in a fresh bed and gown, holding her baby.

'How are you feeling?' Flo asked.

'So happy,' Maggie said, and looked down at her sleeping son. 'He looks so like Ilyas.'

'He does. I certainly didn't smuggle him in under my robe.' Flo smiled. 'He's definitely his father's son. Do you have a name?'

'We like Bassam,' Maggie said, and then looked up at her friend. 'Thanks for being here, Flo.'

'I wouldn't have missed it for the world.'

'After Mum died I never thought I'd love Christmas again,' Maggie admitted. 'But now I want him to know the same magic that I had growing up. I haven't even got him a present…'

'I have,' Flo said. 'I got a few extra bits too and they're all wrapped and waiting.'

Christmas was back.

At least, it was for Maggie.

Flo was beyond tired and looking forward to crawling into bed and pulling the sheets over her head until the day was done.

But that wasn't an option yet.

She didn't want to leave Maggie until she was ready for a long sleep, but that wasn't about to happen as Ilyas returned and informed her that his parents did indeed want to visit.

It was both surprising and nice to see them make an effort. They didn't stay for long, but the Queen even had a small hold of the little baby.

'Congratulations,' King Ahmed said. 'Have you chosen a name?'

Flo watched as Maggie went to respond but Ilyas cut

in. 'We are still deciding.' For whatever reason, Ilyas didn't want to share that particular piece of news just yet, Flo guessed. When the Queen looked over at her, Flo went over and took the baby as Ilyas spoke on. 'I have asked the palace elder, later today, to announce the birth of a healthy son. That is news enough for now.'

The King and Queen left, and with that visit over Maggie sank back on the pillows in relief.

'I think he's starting to get hungry,' Flo said, and handed her back her son. But feeding time wasn't going to happen just yet for there was another visitor.

'Hi, Hazin,' Maggie said, and Flo felt the colour drain from her cheeks.

She simply wasn't ready to face him now, not that she could show it. The last thing Maggie needed was to pick up on even a hint of the tension between them.

It was hard not to show it, though.

Terribly hard, to stand with a fixed smile and pretend that this man had not hurt her deeply.

Hazin came over and gave Maggie a kiss on the cheek and then peered down at the baby.

'He's very cute,' Hazin said, and Flo could hear his attempt to sound bright. He was as pale as he had been on the day he had given the speech. Beneath his eyes there were dark smudges and he looked as if he'd had just about as much sleep as she had.

'Do you want to hold him?' Maggie asked, but Hazin shook his head and politely declined.

'No, thank you. I'm sure he needs his mother right now.'

'Well, I think he'd like to meet his uncle,' Maggie refuted, and held the little baby out.

Hazin rather awkwardly took the baby.

Flo didn't want to look; she didn't want Maggie to get even a hint of the hurt she carried today.

Yet she couldn't not look.

Hazin gazed down at his nephew and watched as he struggled to focus in this very new world, but then Hazin lowered his head and their eyes met. 'Hi, there,' he said to the infant and did not take his eyes from him as he spoke to the proud parents. 'Does he have a name?'

There was no evasion as there had been with the parents. 'Bassam,' Maggie answered, then Ilyas explained why they had chosen that name.

'It means the one that smiles. It is what we both want for him.'

Hazin's face crumpled a touch as he looked at the newborn and heard his new name.

Hazin didn't cry as such, but it was this moment where all could see the pain that he'd kept hidden for so long. Here, today, for a brief moment, it was on show for all to see. Yet for all the pain of the past, there was so much hope for his nephew, who lay so tiny and yet so content in his arms, as if he already knew he was wanted and loved.

Flo went over, only because she was the midwife and could sense he was ready to hand the baby back. The less professional side of Flo could tell he was struggling to keep it together.

'I'll take him,' she said, and as Hazin looked up she saw his eyes were glassy.

'Thanks.'

It was an awkward transition—Flo, who could easily juggle twins on her lap while speaking on the phone, was suddenly all fingers and thumbs as he handed her the little bundle, but of course she clicked into working mode and seamlessly handed him back to his mother.

She could still feel the touch of Hazin's hands on her skin and she had seen the despair in his eyes.

'I'm going to go,' Hazin said. He was a bit embarrassed by the brief slip of his mask so he again offered his congratulations and then left.

As the door closed, Maggie spoke to Ilyas about Hazin and his reaction to the baby. 'He must have been thinking about Petra.'

Flo knew she was brilliant at her job then, because somehow she bit down on a very smart retort about Hazin thinking of Petra at inappropriate times!

And then her anger towards him simply faded.

There was just a hollow ache of sadness.

It wasn't a vague ache, for it gnawed inside her and it felt like hunger.

But hunger she could rectify.

What had happened earlier she could not.

The baby was fed and settled and Maggie too, after a light meal, was ready to sleep. Flo was more exhausted than she had ever been.

Not just physically, she was utterly drained.

'Why don't you go and get some sleep, Flo?' Ilyas suggested.

'I'm going to.' Flo nodded. 'Wake me up when Maggie wakes and if the baby—'

'Rest now, Flo,' Ilyas said. 'We have the palace doctor and there are two nursery nurses. You have been up all night and you need to sleep too.'

Flo nodded, because she knew he was right.

Over the next few days she would be hands on, helping Maggie with little Bassam, but right now she wanted to curl up in bed and just cry.

'Thank you for everything,' Ilyas said, and saw her outside.

She ached, and the walk through the Palace felt like a long one. The high of a successful delivery had faded and the rest of the world, her world, awaited—she just could not bear to face what had happened last night with Hazin.

She would deal with her thoughts later, Flo decided, for right now she was too depleted to think straight.

As she passed the portraits, very deliberately Flo kept her eyes fixed ahead and thought only of bed and sleep. Yet before that she had to ring her family and pretend, for the second year in a row, that everything was okay just so that she didn't ruin their Christmas.

This time, though, she hurt way more than last year.

A married man had been awful.

A grieving widower hurt like hell.

And the sight of Hazin waiting for her as she turned the corner was not a sight she needed right now.

'Not now.' Flo was the one who said it this time and she put up her hands and attempted to just walk past.

'Yes, now.'

'No, because I'm too tired to be polite,' Flo said. 'And I don't want to be mean...'

'I don't blame you if you are,' Hazin said, 'but, please, just hear me out.'

CHAPTER SEVENTEEN

HE GUIDED HER into a room, a library, and she sat there, shivering with cold and tiredness and the hurt of it all.

'I didn't feel for Petra the way I feel about you,' he said, and Flo let out a hollow laugh.

'You've had all night to come up with something and that's the best you can do?'

Flo stood and went to brush past him but he halted her.

'I knew that I was...' He stopped. Hazin was certain he had messed up too much for the plans he had made. 'Flo, I wasn't thinking about Petra.'

'You said her name when you came.'

'*After* I came,' Hazin said, and those seconds mattered. 'Afterwards,' he reiterated, 'I just felt this terrible guilt because I've never felt like that before. I didn't love Petra the way I love you.'

But Flo was so wary and way too used to lies to simply believe him.

She did sit down, though, while Hazin did his best to explain.

'Just before she died, Petra told me that she knew I didn't love her and I can't stand it that she died never knowing love. Because I didn't. Ilyas had again refused to marry and my father had asked me if I was prepared to step up. I said yes. For the first time I didn't feel like a substitute. I did the right thing by my father and I married the bride they chose for me. I did my best and I treated her like the princess she was but—'

'Hazin,' Flo interrupted, 'love doesn't just happen, well, not most of the time…' She had to qualify what she had just said because love *had* just happened to her on the night they had met. 'You married a stranger…' Flo was not a mean person by nature, so she was kind. 'I've seen the way you treat others, I don't doubt you were wonderful to your wife. Perhaps she was just trying to set you free…'

Hazin was quiet as he thought back to those times because that was the type of thing Petra might have done, and then he swallowed as Flo spoke on.

'Maybe love would have grown.'

He nodded.

For in many ways it had.

'You were eighteen when you married, Hazin, and did your best at the time…' Flo shook her head. 'I can't do this now. I need to sleep.'

'Of course.'

She walked away from him, and as she did so his words were playing in her head.

Though the words that were playing on repeat in her head weren't—Petra, Petra, Petra, Petra, Petra. Instead they were…

I didn't love Petra the way I love you.

When Hazin had said *love* had he perhaps meant want?

Or had Hazin just told her he loved her?

And if he had, what on earth was she doing, walking away?

Flo could feel his eyes on her as she entered her

room. She wanted to get away from his gaze so she wouldn't break down and cry and instead could clarify things to herself and think.

But then Flo opened the door and she simply stopped thinking. In fact, she was stunned, because suddenly it had turned into Christmas.

There was a gorgeous pine tree with twinkling lights and all the presents she had wrapped were under it, as well as some she hadn't.

It was bewildering.

Flo stood and breathed in the scent of pine. She looked up at the gold streamers lacing the ceiling. Everywhere she looked it was Christmas—there was even fake snow on the balcony doors.

'Happy Christmas,' Hazin said, and he came up behind her and snaked his hand around her waist, and Flo just leant back on him.

'You did this.'

'No,' he said. 'The staff have been busy.'

'You arranged it, though.'

'With difficulty. When you declined to change rooms I had to think on my feet and somehow get you over to mine so the staff could decorate the room. I filled your stocking, though.'

Flo looked over towards her bed and sure enough there was a red velvet stocking hanging there.

'I believe you're supposed to open your stocking first?' Hazin prompted.

'Absolutely,'

Shaken, Flo walked over to the bed and undid a velvet bow and the stocking dropped into her hand.

'I didn't do the decorations, but I wrapped each gift myself,' Hazin said. 'Well, except for the fruit and nuts.'

He really had! There was a lipstick and a nail varnish and... 'False eyelashes?'

'I had to look up gift suggestions,' Hazin explained.

'Oh, well, thank you very much.'

'There's more,' Hazin said.

Flo smiled as she weighed the stocking in her hand. But then tears filled her eyes because what he had done was beautiful, but the hours before had hurt so very much.

He knew how much he had hurt her, so he took her in his arms and just held her as she tried to work out how it was possible to be so sad and so happy all at the very same time. How to swear never again in one moment, while knowing you were about to dive right back in the next.

'I don't understand what happened, Hazin.'

'Flo, I messed up...' he admitted. It had been the story of his life and Hazin was certain that no apology this time, however heartfelt, could fix it.

'You, really, really did,' Flo said.

'I won't do it again.'

'You might.' She giggled.

For Hazin, it was the most magical sound on earth, so much so that he peeled himself from her embrace and held her as he gazed upon forgiveness.

The right kind.

He just looked at her—and marvelled that she could smile after what he had done. The hint that there would be more chances of getting things wrong helped too.

'I am in love with you,' he told her.

It was so new to them both, such a naked honesty that neither really knew how to deal with a love so exposed.

And so they attempted normality, on a Christmas Day in Zayrinia that had not existed until now.

'The presents under the tree are from your family,' he told her. 'They were delivered last week.'

'So Kumu was lying.'

'On my orders.'

And though usually Flo would be diving under the tree and tearing paper, in bliss to open presents from home, instead she just stood there, those words he'd said still on repeat.

The *I love you* ones.

It was time for Flo to be brave.

She went to the tree and her hand hovered over the two gifts she had bought for him.

'I got something for you too.'

She went for the first, the safe option, yet as she handed it to him there was a flutter of hope in her heart.

He looked at the little card with his name on and opened the parcel carefully.

'Chocolate gingers?' he frowned as he read the box and opened them up. 'I've never heard of them.'

'*Dark* chocolate gingers. They really are the best.'

He bit into one and his smile grew wide. 'They are amazing.'

'I know, I know.'

'They seriously are. Thank you.'

'Once you know how good they are, it's sort of a tradition to eat them every year.'

'I think I can manage that.'

Then she looked at the pile of presents. There was even one from his parents addressed to her. Had they listened to his speech? Had kindness been sown? She looked at the labels on the presents from her family.

To Flo
With Love

Those words were such an unquestionable presence in her life, yet one Hazin had lived entirely without.

It *was* time to be brave.

And so she handed him another present—a slim package. Just an envelope dressed in silver and tied with a bow.

But within it lay her heart.

'This is for you,' Flo said.

He looked at the little card, again with his name upon it, and he undid the bow and then peeled open the silver envelope.

Inside was a ticket to a West End show.

'I've got the other ticket,' Flo told him.

'But it's not until spring?'

'It was the earliest I could get weekend tickets,' Flo said, and then she took a breath. 'And it would give you time to think. If by then you'd missed me…' Then she said the hardest part. 'When I first thought about what to buy you, I was in a department store and decided on some sexy underwear. Something fun and light that could be kept for me, but it wasn't what I wanted…' She looked at Hazin and admitted a truth she had recently learnt. 'I don't speak up enough. I do at work, but in my personal life I'm the queen of pretending that everything's fine and not stating my wants. I've decided it's time that stopped.'

'I agree,' Hazin said. 'So what are your wants?'

'That if we see each other again I want it to be about more than just sex.'

'Such as?'

'I want to go out on a date.'

A first date.

A proper one.

'I would love to go out on a date with you,' Hazin

said, and he looked down at the ticket. It meant so much to be asked for a night out with Flo. 'Perhaps I could take you to dinner beforehand?'

'I'd like that,' Flo said. 'Very much.' But then, at the mention of dinner, her stomach cramped. 'I hate to ruin the romance but I'm so hungry, Hazin, I haven't eaten since…' Flo could honestly not remember when.

It had been her own fault. There had been refreshments discreetly delivered throughout the night, but the knot in her stomach had been placated by endless tea.

Well, no more.

And so, as unsexy as they were, Flo stated her wants. 'I need something to eat.'

'Then I'll call Kumu.'

'But then she'll know you're in here.'

'Flo,' Hazin said, 'I don't care who knows about us. Now, if you are truly starving, open your stocking.'

'It will take more than fruit and nuts…'

'It's not a mandarin,' he said, and picked up the discarded stocking and handed it back.

It felt like it was.

Well, satsuma was her choice of fruit for Christmas Day, but to pick him up on his naming of citrus would be rather splitting hairs when he'd gone to so much effort.

It felt like a heavy fruit for it was soft and round but when she pushed it up through the stocking, Flo found it was, in fact, a squishy, burnt orange velvet ball. Like a luxurious stress ball, it was a work of art, with tiny gold tacks all around and an intricate gold catch.

It was a box of sorts.

Flo did not want to get this wrong.

She did not want to get her hopes up only to be told they were Petra's earrings that he had long kept in a drawer and had hastily wrapped at the last moment so that he could give her a gift on Christmas Day.

She giggled at the chaos of her own mind for she could not quite believe that this moment was hers.

'Why are you laughing?' Hazin said.

'I have a very dark sense of humour.'

'I know you do,' he said. 'Are you going to open it?'

'I'm nervous.'

'Don't ever be nervous with me.'

Hazin wasn't nervous.

Doubt and uncertainty belonged to days prior—delivering a speech while knowing a ring was being made by the royal jeweller, and trying to politely accept commiserations while your heart was soaring for the first time in a decade.

Hazin hadn't just been looking up stocking filler ideas on the Internet, or Christmas decorations either.

He really wanted to get this right, and so when Flo didn't open it he took the box and got down on one knee. 'Florence, will you do me the honour—?'

'Hazin!' Flo screeched, embarrassed, laughing and happy, so happy, all at the very same time. 'Get up!'

'Not till you say that you'll marry me.' He smiled.

'Yes!'

Oh, yes.

And, oh, what a ring.

A diamond that, now she had a Christmas tree, could possibly have been hung on string, or even placed at the top as a star for it was so huge and sparkly.

'See the band…'

She couldn't see, for her eyes were filled with tears, but when she wiped them there were tiny intricate flakes of frost and snow engraved on the white gold band.

She had her white Christmas after all.

It really was the little things.

'I love you,' he told her. 'I have been planning this for a while, and I guess I felt guilty for all that Petra missed out on.'

Now she could see just how the guilt must have played on his mind.

'How do you think her family will react?'

'They were thrilled,' Hazin said, and he smiled at her startled look. 'When I went to dinner the first night, I apologised and they said they wanted me to be happy. That it was time to be.'

'It is.'

'I never intended to tell them about you, but I went over again yesterday. I didn't want them to hear it in an announcement.'

He was, for all his wild ways, the very kindest of men.

'And I had to inform Ilyas too.'

'Am I the only one who didn't know?'

'Pretty much.' He nodded.

'Maggie didn't know.' Flo shook her head as she thought back, because she was certain something would have been said last night, but then she realised what must have happened—Ilyas would have come back from the meeting with Hazin to find Maggie in labour. 'What did Ilyas say?' she asked.

'That he could not be happier for me, as long as you said yes. Flo, I know there is a lot to work out—my brother wants me here but I have told him that I love London too. It is also my home...'

'We'll work it out,' Flo said, for she knew that they would.

'I was going to tell him that for our residence here I

wanted a new area, but now, since you have been there a few times, it is starting to feel like home too.'

There was so much to think about, and so many changes to come for them both, but with the constant of love they would sort it all out, Flo knew.

'I'd better call my parents,' she said, 'given everyone else knows.'

'Why not call them after lunch?' Hazin suggested, as there was a soft knock at the door.

Kumu, with two maids, came in wheeling a huge trolley and they set up the meal at a table.

'Your meal is ready,' Kumu said, and it was clear to Flo that she expected them to come to the table and eat.

'I was just...' Flo started, and then halted, for she could hardly tell Kumu she intended to take her meal to bed.

As well as Hazin!

So she duly took a seat and so too did Hazin. Smiling, Kumu removed the silver cloche covering her plate and Flo stared in disbelief at her meal.

It was a true Christmas dinner.

There was succulent turkey and the trimmings, about which Flo was extremely particular, were perfect.

There were golden Yorkshire puddings and pigs in blankets with a side of bread sauce. Brussels sprouts had been roasted and crisped just as she liked them and there was a glistening cranberry sauce. There were parsnips loaded with butter and what looked like her favourite chestnut stuffing.

Hazin could *not* know all her trimmings.

'Did you speak to Maggie?' Flo asked shaking her head, because although Maggie had joined Flo and her family at Christmas a couple of times, surely she could not have so specifically remembered how things were done.

This was perfect, right down to the willow-pattern-print plate her mum used at Christmas.

Flo was bemused.

Confused.

She took up a fork and tasted the stuffing, and it melted on her tongue.

'That's *just* like my mum's stuffing.'

'Because it *is* your mum's stuffing.'

'Did you ask for the recipe?' Flo said, and then looked at Kumu, imagining the palace chefs trying to get it right, but, no, no one ever could.

For this was perfect.

'Enjoy,' Kumu said, and she left with the maids.

Flo sat facing Hazin and he took her hand.

'I spoke to your father,' Hazin said, 'to ask for his permission to marry you. And then I spoke with your mother and she said she would be delighted to cook dinner a little earlier…'

'This *is* my mum's dinner.' Flo could not take it in, then she remembered her mother on the phone, all tense and too busy to speak—no wonder! 'You had it flown all this way for me?'

'I've been planning this for…' He had been about to say days. About to say how, when the sun had streamed into the cave, he had known this was love.

It had been earlier than that, though.

Hazin thought back to the deserted beach in the Caribbean, knowing she was at the Palace and aching to return, yet wanting the anniversary out of the way first.

And then he thought of the night they had met and how his heart *had* beat faster.

'I've been planning this for quite some time,' Hazin

admitted. 'I got it into my head that I wanted the anniversary over and done with before you and I got together, but I couldn't last. I had Kumu discreetly find out your parents' phone number and on the morning of the anniversary I spoke with them.'

'Kumu knew then?'

Hazin nodded.

She remembered then Kumu standing beside her and translating the speech. How, of late, Kumu had been looking after her that bit more.

'Is that why she asked me to sleep in the west wing? So they could decorate my room?'

Hazin nodded. 'Had you just said yes, we could have avoided—'

'I don't want to avoid anything with you, Hazin. We can face anything. And I loved last night.' She smiled. 'Well, most of it.'

'Call your family...'

She needed to eat but she also needed to speak, so he fed her perfect roast potatoes as she called home.

'Thank you!' the conversation started. 'Yes!' it was all a bit garbled.

Hazin could hear the shouts and congratulations and then they somehow had dinner with her family and ate together across the miles.

And then one of Flo's sisters-in-law asked a question. 'I'm not sure.' She looked over at Hazin. 'Will I be a princess?'

'You'll be a sheikha princess.'

'Oh!' She relayed the information back to her family. 'Apparently I'll be a sheikha princess.'

Hazin loved it that she hadn't particularly cared or known.

For she loved him, he knew.

Then the call ended and they ate the last of their dinner. Flo needed bed, though not to lie down.

'Come here, my bride-to-be,' he said the second she put down her fork.

And suddenly Flo wasn't tired and they tumbled to the bed and kissed. A deep, tender kiss as they peeled their clothes away. Just so utterly thrilled to have found each other. And when they made love, he said her name over and over and over.

'I love you,' Hazin said. It felt so good to say it and deeply mean it.

'I love you back.'

And then, as they lay there in bliss, the oddest thing happened—a large cheer went up outside and they both laughed.

'For a second there,' Flo admitted, 'I thought they were celebrating us.'

'And me. They must have just announced the birth.' And then he looked at Flo, the love of his life. 'As of today, I'm third in line.'

'You've been demoted!'

'It doesn't feel like it.'

Flo looked at her shiny new ring and then at him. 'It's the best Christmas ever.'

He had made it so.

EPILOGUE

STOOD UP!

Hazin had sat alone in Dion's, where they were supposed to be meeting for their long-awaited date, but Flo had not shown.

Now he stood in the theatre foyer as the last call for patrons to take their seats sounded.

He glanced at his phone.

Ten minutes

Flo had sent that text twenty minutes ago!

To the chagrin of her fellow passengers, Flo did her lipstick and make-up on the tube and then ran up the escalators, changing into her heels when she got to the top. Once out on the street she ran a brush through her hair as she raced to get to the theatre.

It was supposed to be a hand-holding romantic night—their official first date!

And yet she was so late they'd missed dinner and would now have to be one of those wretched couples who were shown to their seats late with a torch as everyone pulled in their knees and silently tutted.

But then, there he was, and the world clicked into place with his easy, welcoming smile.

He was wearing a suit and just as stunning to her eyes as he had been on that first night.

'I'm sorry I'm so late.' Flo had been all primed to leave on time, but births worked to their own timeline and at the end of the day she had chosen to stay. 'I couldn't leave her...'

'It's fine. All I ask,' Hazin added as he gave her a kiss, 'is that you're a little more punctual for our wedding.'

The wedding was next week.

It was to be a huge white wedding in London in spring, with all the trimmings and the complication of royal guests too.

Flo could not wait to see Maggie and little Bassam.

Tomorrow was her final day at work and then there was her leaving do to squeeze in.

It was bliss to take their seats and be entertained for a couple of hours.

Except Flo couldn't switch her mind off.

She had just found something out.

It wouldn't be that much of a shock. She had come off the Pill after all, for this very reason.

Flo wanted to work, even after she married Hazin. He had not liked what was happening under his father's rule and had stepped back. Now that the leadership was transitioning toward Ilyas, Hazin wanted to step up.

With conditions, though.

They would have two homes. Flo loved London and her family and that wasn't going to ever change.

But, as Hazin said, it didn't have to. He had practically been raised there too and loved it as much as Flo.

They had found a stunning apartment that would be

their London base, and the rest of the time would be spent in Zayrina.

Flo could still do the job she loved while in London, and just as he pushed for her to follow her path, she pushed for him to follow his.

Ilyas had raised an eyebrow when his younger brother had told him that he would be commencing studying part time.

'We have a lot of ancient heritage,' Hazin had told him. 'I want to better understand it.'

They had decided that while juggling so many balls, yes, they both wanted a baby, so why not throw caution to the wind and see what happened?

She had just found out that it had.

Happened.

They sat in the dark and watched the performance unfold. The show was very good, so very good that the momentous news she had to share suddenly slipped backstage.

His hand was in hers and she loved his easy laugh.

When she had bought the tickets, Flo had thought she might sit through this performance alone.

She well recalled collecting the tickets for a performance that was months away, thinking that she might be the one standing in the foyer, waiting for him to show; that she might sit alone in the dark in the knowledge he did not want her love.

Yet Hazin did want it.

And over and over he showed her that.

It was there in all the little things he did.

The squeeze of his hand at a funny part.

The easy sharing of smiles and chocolate treats.

His love was there waiting, even when she was late.

And she was not nervous to tell him she was pregnant. Simply impatient, for she wanted the world gone, and then to be alone with him at home so she could share the news.

Yet it was only the interval.

'I love intervals,' Hazin suddenly said.

'Why?'

'I get restless.' He smiled that sexy smile. 'I start to smell your perfume. I start thinking of things that I shouldn't.'

'Like what?' Flo asked, assuming he would start the seduction now.

'You're late.'

'I told you, I had a mother who was stressed…' And then she halted as she realised he wasn't referring to her delayed arrival tonight.

In the dark, as her mind had been racing, his had been too.

'How late are you?' he asked.

'Enough for me to take a test at work.'

'And?' he asked.

She nodded.

Just a little nod was all it took.

A little nod that conveyed a huge message and then she felt his arms wrap around her.

It was bliss to be there, wrapped in his arms and breathing in his familiar scent, and to share the happy news.

'Do you know when it's due?' he asked.

It was early days yet, of course, but Flo had naturally worked it out. 'Around Christmas.'

'Well, then, we'd better make sure we have Christmas here,' Hazin said, and all the little flutters of nerves about where the baby would be born were laid quickly to rest. 'It's the best news, Flo.'

'It's not too soon?' she checked, albeit a little to late.

'Not at all,' Hazin said. 'You've been keeping me up all night.'

'You loved every minute,' Flo said. 'And we don't stop just because I'm pregnant.'

'That's very good to know.'

Now there was a choice to be made. They could celebrate the news in the way they did best or answer the call of the bell that was sending them back to their seats.

'Do you want to go back for the second half?' Hazin asked.

She thought for a moment and Flo decided that she did.

'It's our first official date!' she reminded him.

'Do you generally sleep with men on first dates?' Hazin asked, and as always he made her smile.

'Certainly not!' Flo said as they walked back to their seats. 'I'm offended that you asked.'

'Pity,' Hazin said as the lights dimmed. 'Because I've asked for the same table at Dion's and I've booked my old suite in the hope that you're easy.'

It was the very best of first dates.

For love was already sorted. They had the rest of their lives together now.

* * * * *

MILLS & BOON®
Hardback – December 2017

ROMANCE

His Queen by Desert Decree	Lynne Graham
A Christmas Bride for the King	Abby Green
Captive for the Sheikh's Pleasure	Carol Marinelli
Legacy of His Revenge	Cathy Williams
A Night of Royal Consequences	Susan Stephens
Carrying His Scandalous Heir	Julia James
Christmas at the Tycoon's Command	Jennifer Hayward
Innocent in the Billionaire's Bed	Clare Connelly
Snowed in with the Reluctant Tycoon	Nina Singh
The Magnate's Holiday Proposal	Rebecca Winters
The Billionaire's Christmas Baby	Marion Lennox
Christmas Bride for the Boss	Kate Hardy
Christmas with the Best Man	Susan Carlisle
Navy Doc on Her Christmas List	Amy Ruttan
Christmas Bride for the Sheikh	Carol Marinelli
Her Knight Under the Mistletoe	Annie O'Neil
The Nurse's Special Delivery	Louisa George
Her New Year Baby Surprise	Sue MacKay
His Secret Son	Brenda Jackson
Best Man Under the Mistletoe	Jules Bennett

MILLS & BOON®
Large Print – December 2017

ROMANCE

An Heir Made in the Marriage Bed	Anne Mather
The Prince's Stolen Virgin	Maisey Yates
Protecting His Defiant Innocent	Michelle Smart
Pregnant at Acosta's Demand	Maya Blake
The Secret He Must Claim	Chantelle Shaw
Carrying the Spaniard's Child	Jennie Lucas
A Ring for the Greek's Baby	Melanie Milburne
The Runaway Bride and the Billionaire	Kate Hardy
The Boss's Fake Fiancée	Susan Meier
The Millionaire's Redemption	Therese Beharrie
Captivated by the Enigmatic Tycoon	Bella Bucannon

HISTORICAL

Marrying His Cinderella Countess	Louise Allen
A Ring for the Pregnant Debutante	Laura Martin
The Governess Heiress	Elizabeth Beacon
The Warrior's Damsel in Distress	Meriel Fuller
The Knight's Scarred Maiden	Nicole Locke

MEDICAL

Healing the Sheikh's Heart	Annie O'Neil
A Life-Saving Reunion	Alison Roberts
The Surgeon's Cinderella	Susan Carlisle
Saved by Doctor Dreamy	Dianne Drake
Pregnant with the Boss's Baby	Sue MacKay
Reunited with His Runaway Doc	Lucy Clark

MILLS & BOON®
Hardback – January 2018

ROMANCE

Alexei's Passionate Revenge	Helen Bianchin
Prince's Son of Scandal	Dani Collins
A Baby to Bind His Bride	Caitlin Crews
A Virgin for a Vow	Melanie Milburne
Martinez's Pregnant Wife	Rachael Thomas
His Merciless Marriage Bargain	Jane Porter
The Innocent's One-Night Surrender	Kate Hewitt
The Consequence She Cannot Deny	Bella Frances
The Italian Billionaire's New Year Bride	Scarlet Wilson
The Prince's Fake Fiancée	Leah Ashton
Tempted by Her Greek Tycoon	Katrina Cudmore
United by Their Royal Baby	Therese Beharrie
Pregnant with His Royal Twins	Louisa Heaton
The Surgeon King's Secret Baby	Amy Ruttan
Forbidden Night with the Duke	Annie Claydon
Tempted by Dr Off-Limits	Charlotte Hawkes
Reunited with Her Army Doc	Dianne Drake
Healing Her Boss's Heart	Dianne Drake
The Rancher's Baby	Maisey Yates
Taming the Texan	Jules Bennett

MILLS & BOON®
Large Print – January 2018

ROMANCE

The Tycoon's Outrageous Proposal	Miranda Lee
Cipriani's Innocent Captive	Cathy Williams
Claiming His One-Night Baby	Michelle Smart
At the Ruthless Billionaire's Command	Carole Mortimer
Engaged for Her Enemy's Heir	Kate Hewitt
His Drakon Runaway Bride	Tara Pammi
The Throne He Must Take	Chantelle Shaw
A Proposal from the Crown Prince	Jessica Gilmore
Sarah and the Secret Sheikh	Michelle Douglas
Conveniently Engaged to the Boss	Ellie Darkins
Her New York Billionaire	Andrea Bolter

HISTORICAL

The Major Meets His Match	Annie Burrows
Pursued for the Viscount's Vengeance	Sarah Mallory
A Convenient Bride for the Soldier	Christine Merrill
Redeeming the Rogue Knight	Elisabeth Hobbes
Secret Lessons with the Rake	Julia Justiss

MEDICAL

The Surrogate's Unexpected Miracle	Alison Roberts
Convenient Marriage, Surprise Twins	Amy Ruttan
The Doctor's Secret Son	Janice Lynn
Reforming the Playboy	Karin Baine
Their Double Baby Gift	Louisa Heaton
Saving Baby Amy	Annie Claydon

MILLS & BOON®

Why shop at millsandboon.co.uk?

Each year, thousands of romance readers find their perfect read at millsandboon.co.uk. That's because we're passionate about bringing you the very best romantic fiction. Here are some of the advantages of shopping at www.millsandboon.co.uk:

* **Get new books first**—you'll be able to buy your favourite books one month before they hit the shops

* **Get exclusive discounts**—you'll also be able to buy our specially created monthly collections, with up to 50% off the RRP

* **Find your favourite authors**—latest news, interviews and new releases for all your favourite authors and series on our website, plus ideas for what to try next

* **Join in**—once you've bought your favourite books, don't forget to register with us to rate, review and join in the discussions

Visit **www.millsandboon.co.uk**
for all this and more today!